T0198663

BEAUTIFUL LADY

A NOVEL BY
ROBERT PAUL SZEKELY

iUniverse, Inc.
New York   Bloomington

This is a work of fiction. All of the characters, names, incidents, organizations, and dialogue in this novel are either the products of the author's imagination or are used fictitiously.

iUniverse books may be ordered through booksellers or by contacting:

iUniverse
1663 Liberty Drive
Bloomington, IN 47403
www.iuniverse.com
1-800-Authors (1-800-288-4677)

Because of the dynamic nature of the Internet, any Web addresses or links contained in this book may have changed since publication and may no longer be valid. The views expressed in this work are solely those of the author and do not necessarily reflect the views of the publisher, and the publisher hereby disclaims any responsibility for them.

ISBN: 978-1-4401-5962-6 (sc)
ISBN: 978-1-4401-5961-9 (ebook)
ISBN: 978-1-4401-5960-2 (dj)

Printed in the United States of America

iUniverse rev. date: 7/21/2009

LITERARY WORKS BY
ROBERT PAUL SZEKELY

BEAUTIFUL LADY---2009
58 Chapters about a Family of Five and their struggles to
come to the United States from Hungary
in the early 1900's.

SHOWERS OF BLESSINGS---2006
Taylor Free Methodist Church's Poetry Book
Editor & Contributing Poet

THE FIRE & THE FLAME---2004
A Collection of Long & Short Inspirational Stories
One of Xulon's Best Christian Books of the Year 2004

"I REMEMBER...YESTERDAY'S MEMORIES---2003
Short Story Collection

FOUL PLAY---2002
Mystery/Thriller--NOVEL

MURDER BY PROXY---2000
Mystery/Suspense—NOVEL
Writer's Digest --Certificate of Merit

INTERNATIONAL LIBRARY OF POETRY

"YOU COULDA DONE SO MUCH MORE" Poem---2008
Semi Finalist in Poetry Competition
Editor's Choice Award—Oct. '08

WCCAHH'S BOOK, "GOLDEN SNAPSHOTS"

"WOODWARD AVENUE CRUISES..." Short Story--2008
Accepted for publication in their book about the 50's in Detroit, MI.
Article appeared in the local News-Herald Newspapers.

PUBLISHED MAGAZINE ARTICLES

RONNIE'S RHYMES--1998
HAPPY RETIREMENT, HARRY---1996

PUBLISHED NEWSPAPER COLUMNS

SNOW STORY--2008
GAMES WILL GO ON--2006
A PORTLAND STREET CHRISTMAS--2005
BUILDERS OF THE FUTURE—2001
CREATE CLASSY CLUBHOUSE--2001
MY FIRST CHRISTMAS--2000
TRADITION--1998

CONTENTS

CHAPTERS _____

CONTENTS

ACKNOWLEDGEMENTS

TO MY RELATIVES AND CHURCH FRIENDS:
Because of your continued support, I know my writing is being
channeled in the right direction.
A great big THANKS to all of you; without those prayers,
this book never would have been finished.

TO MY NEIGHBORS AND FRIENDS:
A small part of my life, but your hearts are as big as
the great outdoors...thanks, TOM.

TO MY TERRIFIC FAMILY:
For the encouragement from Lisa and Mark, my daughter and
son;
The cards and letters from my sister Elinor,
and my sister-in-law, Jeanette.
You have all given me a lifetime of beautiful memories.

TO MY FABULOUS GRANDCHILDREN:
Ryan, Lauren, Scott & Zac, and Sarah;
You make me laugh. You make me shed tears at times.
I wouldn't have it any other way. Love you all!

TO MY WONDERFUL WIFE:
For your patience and love; you are my inspiration.

DEDICATION

I DEDICATE THIS BOOK ...
> to our Parents and Grandparents
> who came into the United States
> in the early 1900's.

I'VE MADE MANY NEW FRIENDS...
> via E-Mails within the last few years;
> people who love writing for writing's
> sake. I dedicate my new book to this
> group, also.

I'VE TRIED TO HELP ASPIRING WRITERS...
> to develop their love for this craft and to
> encourage them while they hone their
> own unique writing styles.

FINALLY, I DEDICATE THIS BOOK...
> to all of the people who encouraged me
> to start the book; and to those who kept
> after me to finish it.
>> You know who you are.
>> Thanks a million.

"A TRIBUTE "

"Give me your tired, your poor,
Your huddled masses yearning to breathe free,
The wretched refuse of your teeming shore:
Send these, the homeless, tempest-tossed to me,
I lift my lamp beside the golden door!"

These beautiful words are only a part of a poem
written by EMMA LAZARUS in 1883.
It did not receive attention until 1903,
when a bronze plaque of the entire poem
was placed on the inner walls
of the Statue of Liberty's pedestal.

Thanks to *LISA PORTER*
for sending me
this beautiful Tribute

A SPECIAL THANK YOU...

I JUST HAD TO SHARE THIS WITH YOU.
I received a most endearing comment
from my wife Iris one day
during the time it took me to write this book:

"As Bob was writing this beautiful tale,
I felt as if I was Johan Strauss's wife; Johan was
always thinking about his music.
That is what Bob did during the writings of
BEAUTIFUL LADY...
even the title was changed several times.
Enjoy this wonderful up-lifting saga.
I know you will love reading it
just as much as I had
in seeing it become a reality."

IRIS SZEKELY

CHAPTER 1

"What was I thinking?"

JULIANNA:

If I had known it was going to be this difficult to live and work in the United States of America, I would have stayed in our tiny village of Dombrad.

Shortly before the outbreak of World War I, Hungary and Poland, along with other small European countries, were being overrun by the communist regime. It did not matter to us in our small town who these soldiers were, or where they came from; all we knew was that they came into our houses un-announced, took all of our food, our animals, the wine and milk we so dearly needed, and left us with nothing but the clothes on our backs. Any wonder then why we packed up our meager belongings, and even though it took us almost four months, my husband Benjamin and our three children and I finally arrived at Ellis Island in a fancy city they called New York. I should have stayed home.

Everything we owned was in two small velvet valises. Pauley was able to carry the smaller one for me at times, and Benjamin toted the heaviest bag. The two girls carried their assortment of dolls and handmade mementos from our relatives in Hungary.

Our youngest girl, Lizzie, had a terrible cough. Some men in white coats told us we had to wait on the ship until she got better— or if she did not improve, we might have to leave her with a relative that also had to go back with the ship. Our old aunt had a serious disease—we did not know what it was—but they told her she could not come into the country.

Benjamin scratched the brim of his gray felt fedora. The black band around the hat was worn and stained with countless years of sweat and toil. Benjamin loved that old hat. He never took it off his head. He never said much either, but I knew he was not going to leave Lizzie on the ship or send her back. We had come this far; nothing was going to keep us from settling in the United States of America.

He told us to sit along the wall in this great big building in chairs that were older than the ones we left in our kitchen in Hungary. I sat there with the children, luggage next to our feet, our stomachs growling, not saying a word, while Benjamin left us for a while to talk to a white-haired man in a woolly black coat. He was gone for what seemed like hours. A huge clock, with its Roman numerals showing us the time in the brightly-lit building, ticked away the afternoon.

I took the children to the restroom down the tiled hallway while we waited. The room had a tall ceiling with dirty gray globes hanging on long black wires. It smelled of urine and lye soap; otherwise, the toilets were clean enough. We hurried as fast as we could. I did not want my husband to worry if he did not see us sitting in those old rickety chairs.

******

I saw Benjamin coming toward us as the shadows descended over the partitions dividing us from those men in white coats. He motioned for us to pick up our belongings and we went out of the building the same way we came in--from the rear. We followed my husband; Pauley and I carrying the valise, the girls trying to keep up. We were heading back to the pier--the ship. My heart sank as the five of us trudged back toward the bluish-gray dock.

The gigantic sign above this section of the dock read, 'Sight-Seeing--Cruise New York Harbor--Now Boarding'. None of the members in our family could read the words, but it was fun for the children just to see the gulls fighting each other on the top of the black and white sign.

The man with the big woolly coat led the way to the other side of the ship. Benjamin had the heaviest velour case on his shoulder. I carried the slightly smaller bag, while Pauley, Marri and Lizzie did the best they could with their assorted boxes, dolls and toys. He led us down a wobbly ladder to a lower wooden dock. It was quite an adventure just getting all the children and our belongings down to the other level, but one of the woolly-man's crew helped us. He even smiled at us as he took the boxes from the girls, showing his shiny gold tooth. We obediently followed Benjamin up another short wooden ramp, trailing behind him like a row of baby ducklings, onto the boat, toward the waving man in the woolly black coat.

My husband Benjamin was a deeply religious man. I would follow him to the ends of the earth. There, sadly to say, is where we seemed to be heading.

We followed the white-haired man to the opposite side of the small boat. I expected to see others boarding, but as I looked around, I saw that our family was alone on this weather-beaten trawler. I turned to look at Benjamin. He saw the concern in my eyes. The five of us, led by the man in the woolly coat, descended the narrow steps near the bow of the boat. As we were going down into the depths of the trawler, my husband whispered to me in our native tongue. He told me exactly what was going to happen...and where we were going. My face flushed. I felt clammy. But I believed in Benjamin. There was no turning back now.

Once we were below deck, the man in the woolly coat began talking in this language none of us understood, waving his hands, pointing to the walls of the cabin. This made no sense to any of us, until one of his men scurried down the steps and began pulling the bench seats toward the center of the cabin, sliding small panels away from the walls on both sides of the room, just above the cushions. One man took the large valise from Benjamin's hand and put it into the opening. The other man carried the remaining bag and shoved it into the other opening. Now it suddenly became clear to me when Benjamin lifted the two girls in behind the valises. He motioned for me to go with them, handing me a stale loaf of bread and a small piece of dried meat. Benjamin, pulling his felt hat firmly on his head, hid behind the panels on the other side with Pauley. The two men carefully placed the sliding panels back in their original positions. I could hear them grunting as they screwed the panels in place by hand. I could also hear the universal language as one of the crew members pinched his finger when his screwdriver slipped from his hand. Finally, I heard the sound of the last cushion as it was shoved in place with a loud 'thud'.

It was as black as if we had our eyes closed. I could hear Lizzie as she lay next to me, her breath becoming labored, more by fright than the cough. Marri, my older daughter, was so quiet I could neither see nor hear her. I calmly, as best I could, told them what we were trying to do. I cried softly, the tears welling up in my unseeing eyes, when Lizzie said we should say a prayer...now.

******

The trawler pulled away from the dock, its engines straining in reverse. Even in the depths of the hull, we could hear the seagulls, their squawking mixed with the clacking and ticking coming from the engine room. Our hiding place suddenly began a rhythmical quivering. Then it started to fill with the burning smells of gasoline and oil.

As we devoured the meat and bread, I was thinking of Benjamin and Pauley, entombed into the other side of the boat, hoping they had something to eat, too. Sometimes Benjamin would do a crazy thing like that; go without for our sake.

Marri stretched her legs out in the cramped space, leaning against one of the arched timbers. She began humming to herself. I held Lizzie in my arms until she nodded off to sleep. I gently lay her on the soft velvet valise next to me and played with her little fingers, counting them over and over until I dozed off, too.

"AHOY! THIS IS THE UNITED STATES COAST GUARD! THIS IS A SECURITY CHECK! ALL HANDS ON DECK! WE'RE COMING ABOARD!!"

What seemed like an hour or so after we left the dock, I heard the shouts and the horns blowing, but I did not exactly know what to make of it. The shouting I did not like, but the tone of the voice was familiar. Something was definitely wrong. Marri wanted to know what was happening. Lizzie began to whimper and cough. I said another silent prayer for our lost family.

I heard the engines stop, then something hit the side of our boat. Whatever it was scraped the sides of the trawler almost in the same section where we were hiding. I could hear some men yelling at one another. If there had been a hole in this part of the boat, I could have reached out and touched them--that is how close they seemed to be.

Several minutes later, I heard footsteps. Men came down the steps and into the cabin. They talked among themselves. I could hear them opening cabinet doors, tapping on the floors and ceiling. One of the men pulled the cushions away from the walls. I am sure he saw the panels with all the screws fastened to the walls. I heard more talking among the two.

Lizzie must have known how important it was to keep silent; life or death, really. She did not cough. She barely took a breath. I held her close to my body, my eyes wide open, hoping against hope the men would tire in their search.

I heard the men mumble as they shoved the cushions back in place and hurried up the steps. More voices on deck. No shouting now. The engines started up again. I could hear the white-haired man laughing in this uproariously-loud voice that carried all the way down to our secret hiding place. The three of us circled our arms around each other and cried tears of joy and thanksgiving. We were going to be safe now. I was sure of it.

Another two hours passed. Maybe it was more like four or five. Then I heard the footsteps, coming down into the cabin. My heart jumped as the men began pulling the cushions loose and removing the screws from the panels. Lizzie and Marri were fast asleep, thank God. I was startled, then elated, when I heard Benjamin talking to another man in our native tongue.

I was so excited, but I could not understand what they were saying as the engines slowed and the trawler gently hit what sounded like the edge of another dock.

I finally heard Benjamin shout my name through the wall. We were in the United States of America at last!

I spoke prematurely. Seeing the concern on Benjamin's face, I knew we were far from the end of our journey. As I found out later, the journey had just begun.

CHAPTER 2

"Land of the free?"

BENJAMIN:

Now that we were in what seemed like uncharted waters to me, everyone seemed to breathe a bit more normally. Even the engines of the small trawler clicked to a free and easy beat, reminding me of one of my favorite gypsy melodies, 'Igaz E Babbam', a Hungarian Csardas I am sure you have never heard.

The beat of the engines and the smell brought tears to my eyes; maybe it was just because I was staring straight ahead into the Western sun, low on the horizon. I took my hat off and wiped the brim, my forehead and eyes, with my gray handkerchief. It was white when we left our homeland a few months ago.

******

My father Balint, bless his soul, had warned me. But as usual, I would not listen to him. We had heard rumors from the East about the ravaging and destruction of Kisvarda, barely six kilometers from our quiet village of Dombrad, located in the extreme northeastern part of Hungary. Kisvarda, a small town similar in size to our own, had been overrun by soldiers, according to the refugees fleeing to the west. Many people said their homes were burned to the ground. One family told us of seeing unburied bodies at the side of the road. When I heard that, I knew we had to leave. A vision such as that would stay with you the rest of your life.

My father kept telling me that no matter what happened to us, we would still have our home. No one would take our one-hundred-year-old stone house from us. He was right. The soldiers did not take our home.

I had made up my mind to take Julianna and the children to Sweden. There we would take the train into France, eventually waiting our turn for passage to the United States of America. Our Uncle Tobias had written us about the wonders of this New York City and the opportunities available to any hard-working man. I was a shoe-maker by trade. Yes...I was that hard-working man. I prayed we would be in the new country before the end of the year.

My father kept telling me I was making a monumental mistake. "The Czar is not such a bad man", he kept repeating as the war came closer each day.

******

We were roused out of our beds at four in the morning. The soldiers, a dozen of them, charged through our front door. They were yelling at the top of their lungs in a language we did not quite understand...but it had a familiar Russian dialect. The unarmed men ransacked the walk-in pantry, taking all of our food, our milk and wine, including the new crop of potatoes in our makeshift cellar under the floor. We jumped out of the beds, Julianna and I, and comforted the children as best we could. Pauley and Marri, their eyes as big as saucers, sat up in their beds, their mouths gaping wide. Lizzie, thank God, was sleeping soundly, until the youngest soldiers, who appeared to be around sixteen years old, began pulling all the comforters and blankets off the beds. Our handmade bed had a crocheted quilt on it that had been sewn by my deceased mother. The soldiers ripped the blankets off the other beds. Lizzie awoke with a start when her bedding was pulled out from under her. The other soldiers took the wall-hangings, paintings and colorful plates off the walls and threw them in a pile on the floor. They broke our dishes, carried off our pots and pans, and broke the rest of our meager furniture. Lizzie and Marri were crying. My Julianna did not say a word. She was my rock and my foundation. She was always my encourager.

My father could not take it any longer. He waited until the last soldier carried his load out of the house. He limped to the cobblestone fireplace, removed a large stone from its side, and pulled out his shotgun. Before any of us could stop him, he darted out the door, aimed at the first soldier he saw and pulled the trigger. One of the men on the porch slumped forward and fell head first down the steps. Another soldier pulled his Luger from its holster and shot my father, three bullets hitting him in the chest. He held the gun, pointing it at me as I ran out onto the porch. I thought I was a dead man too, but he lowered his pistol and got on his horse. I said a silent prayer for my family as I watched the soldiers ride off with our meager possessions..

I cradled my father's head in my arms. Julianna came out on the porch. She yelled at the children not to come outside. They minded her more than they did me. My father was right...as usual. They would never take his house away from him.

I took off my vest, folded it and placed it as gently as I could on my father's chest, hiding the blood. Julianna put her hand on my shoulder and rubbed my back and neck; she did not know what else to do. Her tears began to fall when she saw the sadness in my eyes. I glanced at my wonderful soul-mate. I felt her strength and compassion, both at the same time. Now I was positive it was time to go to the 'promised land'—America.

CHAPTER 3

"It is no fun being a kid!"

MARRI:

Gretta was carried off by the soldiers. I heard her screaming as she was tied to the back of a large wagon. Gretta knew I was not there to help her. She cried all the way down the dusty road. That was the last time I ever saw my pet goose.

Mama hollered at me and Lizzie not to go outside. We heard the loud 'booms'. Maybe it was Gran'pa's gun, but I was not sure. I started running toward the front door when we heard Mama yell for us to stay inside. Neither one of us ever disobeyed Mama...if we knew what was good for us.

I ran to the window at the side of our house. Lizzie was too short to see what was happening outside. She pulled one of our old kitchen chairs across the floor and banged it against the wall next to me. We could see the soldiers as they disappeared at the bend in the narrow lane. In a few minutes, they were out of sight. Then silence...not a sound coming from our front yard anymore. What was happening?

I shouted to Mama, asking if we could come outside now that the soldiers were gone. She said no. Stay where we were, she said. She sounded like she had been crying. It takes a lot of bad things to make Mama cry. I wondered what was going on out on the front porch. I wondered where Papa and Gran'pa had gone. Where was Pauley? I put my arms around Lizzie. I had a feeling this was going to be a bad day for us all.

I stared out the side window again. The leaves seemed to be made of wood. Nothing was moving. It was too quiet. We had no reason to stay in our old stone house now.

11

*****

My parents were so concerned with us getting into the United States, they could not possibly know what little Lizzie, me and my brother were going through. I will let Pauley tell you later about the nauseating trip across the ocean and our quarters in the steerage section of the ship we traveled on to get to the United States of America. I want to tell you a little about what a beautiful sight I had the privilege of seeing when I woke up on the morning of September 21, 1911.

The people around me called her the 'Beautiful Lady'. At first I did not know who they were talking about until I saw the wonderful Statue of Liberty. I, with the rest of the people around me, cried when we saw it. We felt as if we had just gone into a church--that kind of feeling. Somebody, I do not know who, was reading from a small book. They read the Statue was built originally in 1876. It was supposed to be a symbol of dreams. I think they were right. We started to feel like American citizens before we got off the ship.

We could see people in the harbor waving tiny flags that had red and white stripes with a bunch of stars in one corner. I had never seen this flag before. Someone shouted, "Look! Those are all American flags!" What a wonderful sight.

A tall man with a gray beard yelled as loud as he could, "We go in 'Golden Door' to America!" Other men in black suits, just like Papa's, waved their hands and shouted at the tall 'Beautiful Lady'.

Papa had gone to the front of the ship to get the final instructions from someone called 'The Purser' before we could land. Pauley was running up and down the stairs with his new friends, Karl and Henry, two young German boys. Karl, the older one, liked to pull my braids. He smiled when he did it, too. I could feel my face get warm and rosy. I do not know why.

Mama and Lizzie stayed with me in our fold-up seats next to the iron gates leading down to the steerage section. I did not know what steerage meant--except that we were in it. I found out soon enough.

What seemed like hundreds of people came from the upper decks and began to board boats that were tied to the sides of our ship. They wore fancy clothes and the women all had somebody carrying their belongings. The men smoked cigars and none of them looked like they needed a shave. As soon as one boat was filled, it pulled away and another boat was pulled alongside and more people began boarding. I was getting excited...wondering when it was going to be our turn.

Our turn never came.

*****

Papa came from the front of the ship, two hours after the last boat with all the fancy-dressed people left. From what he could understand, people like us had to go on to the 'Ellis Island', they called it, to be 'processed'. We did not know what was in store for us. But now we knew what 'steerage' meant.

CHAPTER 4

"Princey...I love you!"

PAULEY:

I am not supposed to cry. When you are ten, in our village, you are almost a man, and men do not cry. But I could not help it.

I cried when the soldiers took my pony and shot my dog, Princey. Papa held me around my shoulders--he would not let me go--knowing they were taking everything we owned, including my only possession, a young stallion I was going to train to be my partner. I was going to become a Cossack and ride my horse through the town and let all the pretty young girls wish they could marry me. I could dream with the best of them.

When I lost my two best friends, I wanted no part of Hungary anymore. I wanted to be free from this kind of torture. Little did I realize the tortures that lay ahead.

*****

Yes, the flag-waving was fun, and I wondered why it was taking us so long to get off the ship. There was so much to see everywhere we looked that I could not keep up with the pictures that flashed before my eyes.

A man with a big black mustache was playing a small accordion. Maybe that is not the name for it, but he was singing while he played and the dozen or so men and kids that were gathered around him were all smiling and waving those funny-looking red, white and blue flags. Maybe Mama will let me have one before we get off this ship.

The tallest man looked like our Uncle Tobias who is supposed to meet us in a giant city named New York. We must be getting close to New York by now!

The man stopped playing. One of the other men began waving his hands toward the big statue in the water. The rest of the men began cheering and yelling. I did not know why.

*****

We entered a small harbor that took us to Ellis Island. We heard a bell tolling as the ship was tied to the mooring lines. We were told to form a single file, and follow two tall men in uniforms. Both had badges, a fancy cap and they carried a long stick--why, I did not know. We did what Papa told us to do. We knew better than to disobey Papa...or Mama.

We marched, mostly shuffled, in a never-ending row, into a main hall that looked every bit as big as an acre of land--maybe larger. The room was divided into smaller areas, each with a sign we could not read. At least there were people standing at the entrance to each area, we found out, who spoke the language of the next people in line. These people helped us as best they could, but there was no way to tell for sure. Papa said we were in good hands...but I do not think he believed it any more than I did.

My mind went blank as I stood in the line for hours. We moved forward every once in a while, me shoving the faded velvet suitcase with my foot, until we got to a room called the 'Registry'. There were dozens of old wooden desks with a man at each one. Through an interpreter, Papa tried to answer all the questions the Inspector asked him. Even in this room, there was no chair for Papa to sit. We stood in the background while the man behind the desk, Papa and the interpreter, talked. The three men nodded their heads a lot. Papa talked with his hands like most of the Europeans did, but the man behind the desk did not look up to see his motions. The interpreter did all the talking. We were at his mercy, I found out later.

As I stood in line, I heard the Inspectors ask the same 29 questions to every person who was coming into the country. I got to know all the questions by heart by the time we left the Registry Room.

There was no place to sit down. I stood first on one foot, then the other, taking in the surroundings of this huge building. Just for fun, I took Mama's valise and sat on it, pretending to be a Cossack. She scolded me and told me to stand up straight.

I gazed for what seemed like hours at the massive tiled ceiling. It looked to me to have been made out of tin. The ceiling was a shiny material, but it was full of cobwebs, which floated down and attached themselves to the long black wires that held the large dirty globes of the hanging lights. I started counting the tiled squares, but gave that up real quick.

When we moved forward near the giant wooden columns, I could see where other people had carved their initials into the wood. At first, I wondered how they had the time to do the carving, but the longer I stood there, I knew I could have done it too...but I did not have a knife. That did not stop me. I took my pencil from my inside coat pocket and wrote my name in bold block letters on each column we passed. Mama did not see me do it; she would have yelled and taken my pencil for sure. Mama was very proper when it came to writing on other people's walls.

*****

Papa and our family were taken into a room filled with old men in white coats. We could not understand what any of them were saying. None of them spoke Hungarian, and we did not know how to speak this funny new language, either.

One of them was as bald as Gran'pa and he could hardly walk. None of the old men smiled. They all looked like they wanted to send us back to our little village of Dombrad.

They poked at us with funny sticks and put a black hose all over our bodies. Some of the men had wires stuck in their ears, and they were the ones running the black hose across our chest and back.

Another 'white coat' examined our skin, our eyes, and another man, through our interpreter, wanted us to cough on him. That was so much fun! I did the best I could. Marri and Mama did pretty good, but Lizzie was the one who did the best coughing.

The white-coated men wrote all over stacks of dirty gray paper. Papa and the interpreter began to talk together on the other side of the room. Papa waved at Mama to join them. Mama's face became very sad. She looked over at Lizzie who was standing near the doorway, playing dolls with Marri.

Papa told us we had to wait for him while he went to see a 'friend'. I did not know we had friends already in America. He told us to wait along the wall in the rickety chairs under the clock. He would not be very long, he said. Papa never lied to us; maybe just this once.

*****

I had almost fallen asleep when Papa came down the long hallway of the main hall. He was followed by a man in a big black coat. They both had smiles on their faces. Mama's eyes lit up as she and Papa hugged. We all grabbed Papa's pantlegs; that was our little kid's way of hugging. I still did not understand why we were headed back out of the building, instead of being processed out the front door. I was in line a long time and heard that 98 percent of the people passed--whatever that meant--and this place processed five thousand people a day. I guess we were not to be part of the 5,000 today.

The man in the big black coat waved at Papa to follow him. Our job now was to carry the bags and follow Mama. Marri held tightly to Lizzie's hand as we all hurried after the big burly man.

We went back toward the dock and climbed up a wooden plank, onto a small boat. This probably was a shortcut to the mainland called New York. I was sure of it now. But once we got down below deck, and we were locked behind the walls of the man's boat, my mind began to race with all kinds of wild ideas...all of them bad.

CHAPTER 5

"Where is Gran'Papa?"

LIZZIE:

My name is Lizzie. I am four years younger than Marri, but just because I am small does not mean I do not know what is going on. Mama said for me to keep holding Marri's hand...no matter what. That is what I have been trying to do for the last six weeks.

*****

Every day now, for more days than I can remember, they let us up out of our rooms to play for a little while on deck. I do not see anyone else but the people from what someone called 'The Steerage Sections'. I guess that was our family, too. We got to go outside when the sun was so hot, we had to take off our sweaters. Papa and the other fathers always kept their hats on—no matter how hot it was outside.

I heard one of the men with a badge say the rich people were inside having their 'cocktails', whatever that was. We did not care; we got to play with an old rubber ball and a big stick. It was fun until Karl, our German friend, knocked the ball over the rail into the water. Then we sat on an old carpet and played with Papa's deck of Hungarian cards.

A loud horn blew about one hour later, telling us that we had to go back to the 'hole'. That was what some of the Italian men called the steerage section. It was good for us to be out playing with other children while we were on this ship going to New York; we got to learn so many different languages. We could say 'Hello' in six different ways. Marri seemed like she was closer to fourteen years old on some of those days. All I know how to say is 'Good Day', which means 'Yo Napput' in Hungarian. That was hard enough for me to learn. After all, I am only eight.

Henry, Karl's younger brother, tried to teach me some easy words in the German language. No matter how many times I said the words, they still came out sounding more like Mama talks. I finally learned how to say 'Lizzie' in German...but now I forgot it. But I am a smart little girl; my real name is Erzsebet in our tiny village of Dombrad. In the new world, it means Elizabeth. I like the sound of my new name better. I laughed when I told the new name to Henry. He tried and tried, but he could not say my fancy American name.

We have been on this ship for a long time now. I still do not know why Gran'pa did not come with us to the new place they call America. Maybe he does not like to ride on big boats that go up and down all day long; it even gets me sick some times.

Papa said he was not sure how long it would take to get to the new country, but I can tell you right now...even if I am only eight... it will never be as good as it was in our little town of Dombrad.

*****

When I saw the bad men tying Marri's goose to their wagon, and heard it honking and crying like a baby, I ran into our tiny closet near the front door. At first, when I closed the door, I was surprised the coats did not cover my head like they usually did when I hid in the closet. Then I remembered that the soldiers threw all of our clothes on the floor, in a pile, and took what they wanted. The young blonde soldier took my green and white dress that Mama made for me last year. The rest of our things they burned in our front yard.

I did not have a warm jacket to cry into, so I covered my eyes with my hands and cried; not because the goose was gone, but for Marri. I knew she was in the woods behind the house, crying because the soldiers took Gizza. She loved that goose even more than me. At least that is the way I felt sometimes, but not today.

I felt sorry for Pauley, too. It happened so fast; our dog Princey and his pony-- gone. I tried to hide Tweet Tweet, the pretty tiny birdie Mama gave me for my last birthday. I did not think the bad men would be so mean. Tweet Tweet is dead, too.

I saw Mama picking up some of our clothes from the pile in the yard. The coats and jackets did not get burned. Papa's old shirts and Pauley's pants looked good enough for them to wear again.

Papa's black suit, the one without any holes in the elbows, lay on the ground next to the wooden stump we used when we played hide-and-seek. Mama picked it up, shook off the dirt and shoved it under her arm. The pants were covered with dirt, but I knew Mama could get them as good as new.

Marri, with tears dripping down her face, came running from behind our favorite hiding place--the big weeping willow tree. She buried her head in Mama's apron.

Mama did not say a word about Gran'pa. I did not ask her where he or Papa went. All they told me was that Papa had taken him to the back of the house...to show him something, I guessed. They were gone for a long time. I did not care; I was too busy crying about Tweet-Tweet and Princey.

When I saw Mama put her arms around Marri, I ran from the house toward them and threw my arms around my sister and Mama. I was safe now.

But I did not care if I ever saw this stone house again.

CHAPTER 6

"Why, Benjamin—why?"

JULIANNA:

I am not sure if this is the second day, or the third, since we left the dock with the man in the woolly coat. We are seeing less and less of the tall buildings as the trawler makes its way westward. All during our first day, after we left the port near Ellis Island, we were anxiously looking for the wonderful American dock where we would land and see our Uncle Tobias waving at us. Not any more.

But I was happy to hear that one of the crew members could speak a little bit of Hungarian. He was able to calm the girls, and I thought I would be able to find out where we were headed. I was wrong; he was told by the man in the woolly coat not to talk to me...or Benjamin. He kept his word.

If we looked over the trees, every once in a while we could still see some of the very tall structures, but only when we were at the back of this old boat. I know, since we left, we have been going away from the morning sun, and have been following it until it sets in the early evening.

*****

I went down into the cabin near the back of the trawler and picked up Marrie and Lizzie's clothes. The girls had left them on top of a wooden trunk before they went to sleep. I washed the two dresses that the soldiers tried to burn in our front yard. While they were asleep, I carried the dresses and their underwear up on deck to dry.

23

Marri was going to wear her black cotton dress again today, and Lizzie had the brown one. I had made them each a white bow for the dresses during our trip. I wanted the girls to wear something pretty when we came into the United States a few days ago. They never had a chance to take the bows out of the small velvet valise.

Springtime is the best season to come to America. Uncle Tobias kept telling us for two years after he arrived in the United States. Benjamin, for whatever reason, never told me why it was the best time. I still do not know, but I think I almost have the answer. I will know for sure within the next few days.

When the sun was setting, low on the horizon, I asked Benjamin if we are going to see Uncle Tobias soon. He looked at me with that blank expression of his. He took off his hat and wiped the inside band with his gray handkerchief. He put the hat back on his head. He always did that when he wanted a minute to think of an answer before he spoke. Benjamin shook his head and said no...we would not be seeing him for at least two weeks—maybe longer. I knew better than to ask any more questions. I did not want to add to his worries. I made up my mind not to mention Uncle Tobias's name to Benjamin again.

*****

I wondered why we had to stop every night shortly after the sun went down. The trawler chugged and blew thick black smoke into the air as it made its way into the edges of the low-lying trees along the banks of the densely populated terrain.

I tried to find out where we are going from the one man who could speak our language, but he just smiled at me and said, "Hagyj bekeben"! I do not have to tell you that in English that means 'let me alone'.

The trawler's engines stopped. The boat had nestled into a grove of blackish green trees. I thought I heard its bottom scrape along the sand at the edge of the river. The boat seemed to have settled itself in for the night. Not unlike us, I thought.

Three men from the crew hurried from the front of the boat. They opened a large storage bin that was above the lower cabins.

The first two pulled out a large heavy piece of canvas and pulled it toward the front side of the boat, facing away from the shore. The canvas had been painted to look like trees and bushes. The third man began opening up the canvas and started to lay it over the side of the boat, covering it from front to back. Another piece was draped over the cabin itself. This became a ritual every night. It was as if they had to put the trawler to bed at the end of the day.

I asked Benjamin why the man in the woolly coat and his men had to do this. He told me not to worry...it was best that I did not ask any more foolish questions.

CHAPTER 7

"Is this our new country?"

BENJAMIN:

I do not know why, but I did not think of making a Log or a Journal when we got on this trawler with the woolly man and his crew. He told me it would be only a few days more, so I took him at his word. That was another mistake; I am almost sure of it by now.

At the end of the third day since leaving the harbor at Ellis Island, I thought it would be a good idea to make a map; a rough drawing of the river and all the curves and bends that we have been going through. I began to scribble on the back of a booklet of parchment paper I found on a crate near the engine room. The paper sheets looked like the directions for repairing broken parts. I could not read the words, but I felt I needed to say a silent prayer now. I took off my hat and wiped the inside with my grey handkerchief, praying that the trawler did not need this book while we were on our way to America.

*****

Two days later, I had filled up one of the pages with lots of curves that looked like a bunch of esses, going backward and forward. I made quick sketches on the paper when I felt we made another turn, and darkened it in when I knew I was alone. When I finally had a chance to connect the three pages of my hand-made maps, I could see that even though we were always going from one side of the river to the other, then back again, we were always heading West.

In the wee hours of the morning one day, I saw a large sign

above the trees on the opposite side of the river. It had dirty black letters that spelled out C-A-N-A-. The rest of the word was hidden by a large oak tree. I wondered what that meant.

I noticed this week, that the weather started to get a bit cooler, too. I thought we might be going further North also. I was just guessing; it was Gran'Papa who could tell you what the weather would be like tomorrow by looking at the Western sky. I wiped my brow and wiped away the tears as I thought of my father, buried in the back of his old stone house in Dombrad.

*****

At first, I did not know why we had to go from one side of the river to the other shores all the time. Then, one night, it all became clear to me.

The man who could speak Hungarian confided in me when I asked him about the searchlights on the white patrol boats. He told me that the boats were looking for illegal aliens trying to come into the United States of America without 'Passports'...whatever that meant. Every night, they were trying to hide from this boat; they called it the 'Coast Guard', and the man in the woolly coat was doing a marvelous job of not being discovered.

They had maneuvered the trawler to shore as usual. I watched them take the large pieces of canvas out of their storage areas, and watched as they covered the top parts of the boat. The hull was painted in greens and browns to match the shoreline. The spotlights from the boat played over the low-lying branches that covered part of our trawler. The hull blended in with the foliage at the side of the river and the canvas-covered decks above. In the darkness, the trawler looked like part of the scenery. The man in the woolly coat must have been doing this for a long time; he had all the details down perfectly. The old weather-beaten trawler, I am sure, looked invisible to the searchers.

This regimen always confused me. Why were they doing all of this extra work?

Yes...why do the extra work—unless it was not legal. I finally figured out the answer. We were being taken into the United States of America and they were doing it against the law! That must be the answer! What will I say to Julianna and the children? Can we enter the country knowing that we are going to be illegal aliens?

I thought of Lizzie. I did not want to go back to Hungary because of her cough. We must stay together as a family! This may be the only way we could get into America and to find Uncle Tobias. We will have to do what the man in the woolly coat says...right or wrong. We have no other choice now.

*****

I do not know the Hungarian term for 'Tributary', but I believe we have seen most of them during this trip.

The man, Johan, who speaks a little Hungarian, told me that we are not the first family the woolly man has brought into the United States. He also told me during the Spring season, many of these little tributaries, that flow into the larger streams, never appear on any maps. As the seasons change, like in late summer or early fall, the waters we have been traveling on so far cease to exist.

Who was I going to believe? Do I put my trust in what this stranger tells me? Can I truly trust this man in the woolly coat who will not even tell us his name? Or do I put my faith in something higher...which is what Julianna would tell me to do.

I kept my secret from Julianna. I will not tell her until I must. I need some time to make the right decisions. I will take her advice and take some time to pray about this problem. We have come this far...we will be all right. I know that is what Julianna would tell me.

The man in the woolly coat told me not to worry about how we are going to pay him for bringing us into America. That was a bad sign for our family, too. I wondered now if Uncle Tobias was an illegal alien.

*****

I watched Marri and Lizzie playing on the other side of the

trawler. I could hear them both giggling when they pretended to be a couple of parrots.

The setting sun was trying to force its way between the low-lying trees along the shoreline. It was a beautiful view of our new country. We will be getting off this boat soon.

Sometimes I am not so sure.

That is why I need Julianna. Bless her.

CHAPTER 8

"Fun with Lizzie."

MARRI:

I used to be small like Lizzie. I know what it is like to live in a little-girl world. It can get to be scary sometimes.

Mama said I should be a mama to Lizzie while we are on this boat. She told me she had to keep Papa happy while we are going to see Uncle Tobias. They told me it might be one or two days more. I am not so sure about that.

I could see the worried look on Papa's face. He smiled at me when he knew I was looking at him. Many times during the day, I could tell he was keeping something from me, Pauley and Lizzie.

Mama was always smiling…nodding her head up and down as she walked from one side of the boat to the other. Most of the time, she stayed below deck. That is where Papa and the man in the woolly coat told her to stay.

I can see the boat going from side to side all day long, too. I know Papa and Mama know when the boat stops at night and the men cover it up…just like Mama does to me and Lizzie.

*****

Mama wants Lizzie to take a nap in the middle of the afternoon, so she would not be crabby by the time she has to go to bed. When she takes her nap, I try to go to sleep, too. If I do that, Mama lets me stay up a little later after my sister falls asleep. Most of the time I fool Mama…but I think she knows.

As I lay on the bumpy mattress across from Lizzie, I dance the Csardas in my dreams, dancing to the beat of the boat's engines. I pretend I am with my friends, dancing at the Hungarian Festival in our little town of Dombrad, eating bacon-bread sopping with tiny slices of charred bacon. Yum! Yum!

I have so much fun when that happens, sometimes I sleep longer than Lizzie. She jumps on my mattress and wakes me up. She wants to play one of her favorite games.

I can keep Lizzie happy most of the time. She likes to play games during the long afternoons. Some of the games she enjoys are the 'Counting & Color' games.

Sometime we start counting the trees with red leaves. You get extra points if the tree had flowers on it. One time the boat stopped under a tree that had big red apples hanging right over the top of our trawler. One of the men lifted Lizzie up so she could pick some of the apples for us. She was laughing so hard, she dropped most of them on the deck. Even Papa almost smiled. That was a happy day.

Another favorite game both of us liked to play was the 'Birdie' one. The first person to see a bird, flying or in the air, got five points for each bird. We played the bird game until one of us got to 50 points. Pauley liked this game most because he won almost every time we played it.

Mama came up the stairs from the cabin and told Lizzie to go and take her dress off so she could wash it. She said we should be getting near the place where we have to get off the trawler, and she wants us to have our dresses nice and clean. She said you never know who you will see when we get to the United States. Pauley laughed and told Lizzie she better hide or the big birds would eat her for supper. Mama sent Pauley down to change his clothes, too.

I was the oldest. Mama told me I had to wash my own dress and the long black cotton stockings that I wore. Lizzie could not clean her own shoes either, so I cleaned her shoes when I washed mine. I hurried to get these chores done as soon as I could. I did not want Mama to be mad at me...not if I wanted my supper.

*****

When I heard all the engines stop, I knew it was time to pray. Mama made sure we learned how to say our prayers. She still helped Lizzie say a real easy one. I make up my own prayers now. After all...I am almost thirteen.

Everything is so still. I am laying on my back staring up at the dirty ceiling. I can hear myself breathing. Sometimes, I almost stop breathing. I do not like it when that happens.

CHAPTER 9

"The Grand Ballroom!"

PAULEY:

We ran down the dirty wooden floors of the steerage section as fast as we could. The three of us tried to slide into the life preserver on the end wall with a loud bang. My two new friends, Karl and his brother Henry, made the biggest noises. This was a new game that we played almost every day. We got tired of just running around from one end of the long hallway to the other. We pretended we were escaping from the ship's jail; the first kid to the end of the hall got to go free. That makes you run for your life, yelled Karl. He was right!

We had not seen the sun for several days...maybe it was more than a week. If I asked my Papa, he would know exactly how long we have been on this old ship, buried below in what everyone called 'The Steerage'.

Karl was the oldest of all the boys in this part of the ship. Do not forget, we were four floors below deck. Karl was 14 years old; almost a man in our little town of Dombrad. His 12–year-old brother did as he was told—otherwise, he knew the anger of his older brother. The three of us had a good time down in the depths of this old ship. Sometimes, they ganged up on me, but I did not mind. It was more fun than trying to play with Lizzie or Marri.

They knew how to speak a few basic words of Hungarian, and I understood a tiny bit of Polish, so we got along without any big problems. You know how boys are.

One of the crew members came down the stairway in the middle of the long hallway. He yelled at us and chased us away.

We knew that, every day, it was his job to check the locks on the three iron folding doors. We could tell by the way the Steward did his job that he was bored and tired of this chore. He did not notice that we had wedged a small stick into the side of one of the doors, to keep it from locking into the left edge of the wall. We were watching him from behind the worn leather couch, about twenty feet from the Steward. He hurried up the stairs and began whistling a funny Irish tune.

We waited until we were sure he was gone. Karl was the first one to the door. He listened for a minute, then slid the door quietly to the side. The three of us hurried up the stairs, hoping, and I was praying, that no one would see us before we got to the main deck. We tiptoed quietly up the four levels of rickety stairs. Thank heaven...we made it!

*****

Karl pushed the swinging door open to the deck. Henry and I had to cover our eyes for a moment. The bright sun shining through the windows of the long carpeted hallway that led to the deck almost blinded us.

I saw the giant brass and oak doors ahead. A woman in a white flowered dress, holding the hand of a cute little girl about my age, went ahead of her husband through one of the swinging doors. The three of us hurried to the door and went inside. We tried to pretend we were part of his family. It seemed to work.

Once inside, we walked slowly and very erectly, then stood behind a group of men who were standing in front of a giant staircase. They all had a different kind of drink in their hands. All of them were so busy talking and gesturing, they did not even notice us.

We looked up the staircase that seemed to wind in a giant circular fashion so far in the sky that we could not believe our eyes! Henry's mouth was wide open, staring at the carpeted stairs that disappeared about four stories above us. Karl's eyes bulged out more than mine. I was sure of it!

The stairway was carpeted in colors of green, blue and gold, with black and white swirls in them. I could see a giant picture of a man in a black uniform way up on the first landing. Maybe he was the captain of the ship. The painting was in a thick gold frame; real fancy, with curved sides. It was even bigger than Karl!

The landing at the very top seemed to go up into the sky. It was made of rounded glass, with flowers painted all over it. Part of it looked like mountains, going up as far as I could see.

Then I began to cry softly...at first. I could not keep it in. Tears streamed down my face as I wiped them with my dirty sleeves.

"Why are you crying," asked Karl. He put his hand on my shoulder, bent down toward me almost like a Papa would do for his son.

At first I had no idea why I started to cry. Then, I was startled by this strange revelation; all of a sudden, I understood. I was crying because I knew that my Mama, Papa and sisters, would never be able to see something as beautiful as this Grand Ballroom.

I wondered about this for as long as 10-year-old boys usually wonder about things; Heaven must be a more beautiful place than this. It is way higher than the Grand Ballroom.

Karl pulled a wrinkled handkerchief from his back pocket and gave it to me. I wiped my eyes and blew my nose. Henry just watched with that wide-eyed look of his.

We all looked at each other as the Fog Horns sounded three times...the signal to go back down to our least favorite place; the Steerage Sections.

CHAPTER 10

"Watching the trains."

LIZZIE:

Marri has been playing with me for almost three days now. We are having a lot of fun, but sometimes she looks out at the river and is quiet for a long time. I wonder then if Mama told her to keep me busy so I would not bother her. Mama has not looked very happy now since we got on this boat. She looks sad and worried. I thought only Papa had to do that.

We played a lot of new games since we started going down this river. Marri, and even Pauley, made up games as we went along. One of my favorites was finding the big green trees with the giant red berries on them. I was really good at that game. But Pauley got mad when he saw Marri pointing them out to me, so I could win the game. Finally, Pauley went down into the cabin and went to sleep. The two of us leaned back into the old wooden bench and stared out at the water. I did the staring...Marri closed her eyes and pretty soon her chin was touching her black dress. I started to play with Nana, my doll.

*****

Dolls are okay to play with, but only for a little while. I put Nana in Marri's lap and went to the other side of the boat. The sun was going down; it seemed to be floating on top of the water. Mama and Papa were getting our supper down below. This was a beautiful time of the day.

I came around the corner of the cabin and saw four of the men jumping into the water. One of the men, the tall one, did not have any clothes on! I stopped…and I could feel my mouth drop open and my eyes seemed to pop from my head. It was getting colder by the minute, but the men were yelling and shouting and having a wonderful time.

I did not see the big man with the woolly coat, or the only man that talked to Papa one day. Maybe they were busy driving the boat.

I was wishing I knew how to swim…but not with those scary men!

I ran to the other side of the cabin. I stopped when I saw a long train going around a bend in the forest. The shiny train was going along the edge of the river. The freight train whistled again as the coal cars came into view. I could see the fancy people in the dining cars through the big windows. The yellow lights were snuffed out as the sun hid behind the hill of mud and broken pine branches.

I got tired of watching the water. By that time, the train got so small it looked like a toy I could reach out and play with. I thought I should go and wake Marri up so she would not think she was a bad babysitter.

*****

I whispered as loud as I could in Marri's ear. I held my hands around her ear trying to make a tunnel. I think she woke up more from my spit than my whispering.

Mama and Papa were not in the cabin. Our food for supper was on the table. Pauley told us they had gone upstairs to see the man in the big black coat. He said Papa looked mad and Mama was not happy, either. I was hungry, and so was my sister. We sat down and ate the same soup and stew we have eaten for the last several days. We did not dare say a word about the food. Mama and Papa had enough worries of their own. We could be good kids if we tried.

Pauley finished his food before we did. He said Papa told him to go straight to bed. He told us we should do the same…if we knew what was good for us.

Marri washed my face and hands. I went to go pottie in the big bucket in the corner. Marri tucked me into bed, helped with my prayers, and she even gave me a hug and a kiss. I guess she was trying to be a Mama. I liked it.

Marri told me to think about all the things that I love. Before I knew it, I was almost asleep.

*****

I was getting so tired. I could hardly keep my eyes open. That was good…that is what I have been trying to do.

Mama said it would not be a long time before we got to America. I think Marri said it was about three days ago when we got on this boat. Papa told me it might be tomorrow when we get to America.

I will be so happy when we get off this boat. Then I can play in the dirt again.

CHAPTER 11

"New York at last!"

JULIANNA:

It was a little before the sun came up when I noticed that the engines had stopped. For some reason, the old trawler did not stop at the shorelines last night like it has done for the past several days. But I remember the constant clicking and ticking, even though it kept on for hours; it helped me fall back into a peaceful sleep sometime in the middle of the night.

As I looked out the tiny round window of the boat, I could see the white sun peeking over the water on the other side of the river. Right before my eyes, the sky began to turn a very pale yellow, then, almost before I knew it, the color changed to a beautiful shade of pale orange; the lightest I have ever seen. As I stared at this wonderful presentation from God, a white line flashed across the horizon. I was so surprised to see the sun coming up in this manner. For a moment I felt as if I was in Heaven, looking down at our little world.

I was startled out of my daydreaming. The engines stopped. They began making hissing and popping noises. It sounded like the boat was so tired and ready for a very long rest. Just like me, I thought.

I heard Benjamin coming down the steps. He was dressed in his black suit, wearing his faded gray felt hat. He leaned over my cot and told me to get dressed as quickly as I could; then I should wake the children. He did not say why. Benjamin told me to have everyone pack all their belongings, but to stay in the cabin. He would call if he needed me, he said. I did not know if that was a good sign…or a bad one.

******

The children were walking around in a daze. It was so early in the morning Lizzie wanted to know why we were not going to have breakfast before we went up on deck. Then Pauley began to look for his cap and the whistle Karl gave him. I helped Marri find the shoes that Pauley had hidden under her metal cot.

As soon as I dressed Lizzie, I put everything we owned in the center of the small room. When I saw what we had on the floor, I was amazed at how little we brought from our old country. Maybe that was a blessing, I thought to myself. There is good in everything...yes?

*****

What seemed like an hour later, Benjamin hurried down the steps of the cabin. He was happy to see that the children were dressed, sitting in a row on top of the gray mattress on the other side of the room. He told me to keep the children and all of our things right where I had them, then for me to wait until he returned.

Benjamin went over to each of the children and hugged them. He hugged Lizzie first. She dropped the doll when he picked her up ever so tenderly. Lizzie wrapped her little arms around Papa's neck, dirty blonde hair falling into his collar, just like she used to do with Gran'Pa. Marri tried to act a lot older. She hugged Benjamin around his waist. He knelt down and kissed her on both cheeks. Then he told the girls how much he loved them. He shook Pauley's hand and just nodded his head. Pauley looked up at his Papa and smiled. Inside, I think he was glad Benjamin did not give him a kiss!

Benjamin came over to my side of the cabin, took off his dirty hat and gave me the biggest hug that I have ever gotten from him in my whole life. At first I was surprised...then I became very worried. What was making my Benjamin act this way? Was he going to leave us? Or was he planning to send only the four of us to find Uncle Tobias? Crazy mixed up thoughts began running through my mind. Was this how we were to come into the United States of America? Was I to be greeted by Uncle Tobias in my oldest dress and shawl?

Benjamin told the children to wait in the cabin until it was time to get off the trawler. I was to come up on deck with him because he wanted me to see this beautiful new country. I was to come back downstairs later and bring the children up on deck.

I could not believe it!

Were we in New York City at last?

*****

The edges of the trawler were scraping the low-lying leaves of what looked like a one-hundred year old tree. If this was New York, I was not very impressed.

I heard a lot of shouting and talking among the men on deck. I was surprised when I saw the big man without his black woolly coat. He had on a green coat that came down below his knees. It had a big collar with two pockets. A green woolen cap was pulled down over his ears. He smiled at me for the first time since we got on his boat. I was not sure if that was a good sign. As usual, I had too many other more important things to think about. I knew Benjamin, and our God, would get us through this ordeal.

The man in the green cap pointed at his men. I stood and watched while two members of the crew unhinged a large wooden platform that was hung on the side of the wheelhouse. It was made of heavy two-inch thick boards and seemed to be about ten feet long.

They carefully laid it on the edge of the trawler. Then one of the younger men positioned the platform and locked it into two rusted fasteners that were the width of the boards. Two other crew members grabbed the ropes that were tied to the platform and pushed it away from the trawler, making it swing in a large half-circle. The platform fell gently on a large pile of black dirt next to the shore.

At last! We now had a bridge to the New World! Thank you, God!

Benjamin hurried toward me from the front of the trawler then asked me to go below once again and stay with the children. The big burly man wanted to speak to him one last time before we got off the boat. It would not take long. Benjamin said our worries were finally behind us.

******

I hurried down the steps. Benjamin told me to stay with the children until he came to get us. As soon as I got to our cabin, I told the children to form a circle. We stood, held hands, and said a prayer for Benjamin and the crew of the trawler. The children could barely contain themselves; they wanted to see their Uncle Tobias as soon as they could. They all had those funny smiles on their faces that only children can make.

I stood between the girls, holding on to their rough little hands. I squeezed their hands more than I usually did. They knew our prayer was a very important one right away. They all looked up at me. Then we all closed our eyes. I was glad we did that; I did not want them to see the tears flowing down my cheeks. Something told me it would be a long while before we were to see our Uncle Tobias again.

CHAPTER 12

"Where are we going?"

BENJAMIN:

The young man, who could speak a little Hungarian and also served as our much-needed interpreter, grabbed my arm as soon as I approached the wheelhouse. I was hurrying to meet with the owner of the trawler one last time. The young man informed me that I was to see him on the other side of the platform. He wanted to have our farewell meeting with me on solid ground. I followed him to the North side of the boat.

I was led across the wobbly ramp. For the first time in a week, we were on land once again. What a glorious feeling! My young friend grinned at me and nodded his head up and down. That seemed like a good sign. I was sure now that we would see Uncle Tobias very soon.

The owner, now wearing a green coat, was waiting for me behind a grove of birch trees not too far from the shoreline. Two of his men were standing behind him. He smiled at me, showing his shiny gold tooth and folded his arms across his barrel chest. He blended in perfectly with the bright green leaves of the trees that seemed to encircle us.

I stood facing him, wondering why we did not see the city of New York. We did not see ANY city!

Last night I asked Julianna if she could clean the dirt off the elbows of my black suit. I wanted to look my best when we saw our American relatives in this new country.

The owner reached out and shook my hand. He grinned and held up a dirty wrinkled map. He looked at our young man and spoke to him in what sounded like German to me. I understood some of the words. I did not like what he was going to tell me. I was glad Julianna was not with me now.

The young man, as best he could, finally explained to me that this is where our trip would end. We are now in Canada, he said. Canada is north of the United States. Not too far away from New York City. But the trawler will not be able to take our family any further; too many Coast Guard boats patrolling the rivers in this area. He said if those boats found out that our family was trying to get into the United States illegally, we would all be sent back to Hungary...or to jail!

The young man also told me that the owner of the trawler would have his boat taken away by the authorities. He was not going to risk losing his only means of survival.

I could see that the map had a small circle drawn on it in pencil. It was the location of where we are now. It will be up to me to find our way back to the United States. Then he told me it was not too far away—perhaps a day or two.

In the distance, I saw the roof of a barn and an old house. They seemed to be less than a half-mile away. The dirt road at the edge of the woods led South, away from the river. I did not see any other roads or houses. What I saw was empty land and meadows. In front of me was the large river that we were on, with several streams running from it. As I looked toward the West, it reminded me of our native land in Hungary. This Canada had many more mountains than we have in our country...otherwise it was very pretty.

I reached for the map. I did not tell anyone I had made my own map for many days. Perhaps I would be able to find our way to the United States if we had horses and a wagon.

The owner pulled the map back and shook his head from side to side. He held up his other hand and said 'Nein!' in his native tongue. The sun was low on the horizon by now. He squinted as he looked at me and shouted, No! No!

He spoke to his young interpreter. He kept pointing at himself, then back to me. The young man said the owner wanted to be paid for bringing me and my family to this country, even though he could not take us all the way to the United States. This was the best he could do, he insisted.

I told him I only had $100. in American money. That was all Uncle Tobias sent us and that it would be enough for us to meet him in New York City. I took the money from my pants pocket and held it out for one of the men to give to the owner.

The man closest to me grabbed the money out of my hand. The owner became furious! He told his men to search me. He yelled in German that I must have more money on my person than that small amount! Search me…NOW, he yelled. My young man tried to calm him down, but he could not do it.

*****

One of the men stripped me of my coat, and the other threw my hat into the brush next to the largest birch. The taller of the two tore into the lining of my coat, trying to find any money that Julianna might have sewn into it. The owner was watching his men with fire in his eyes.

The other man pulled at my shirt, ripping two buttons off the front of it, exposing my hand-made money belt. As you might know by now, I am a shoemaker by trade. I sewed this canvas belt with black stitching, and expected it to last our family for a long time. I did not know people were so cruel in this new country. The man with the gold tooth grinned when he saw my money belt. I could see the dozens of dollar signs in his wild eyes.

A member of his crew ripped the money belt from my waist. He laughed as he handed it to his Captain. The owner raised the belt above his head, swinging it around and around his green wool cap. He smiled, then yelled some loud phrases in German that I remember hearing when I was a young lad; words that I would not repeat in front of my children.

He was even more upset when he discovered my belt contained only $200.in Hungarian and $50. in American money.

*****

The man with the gold tooth came down the wooden ramp and stomped his feet firmly into the yellow clay of Canada. He glared at me and shook his head from side to side. He had a very serious look on his face as he put the dirty map in my coat pocket.

Then, all at once, his entire attitude changed. Perhaps he suddenly recalled the suffering his own parents had to endure for the past forty years in Germany. A very faint smile crossed his lips.

He shook my hand and began talking to me in his native language for almost five minutes. I understood only a few of the words. He told me, through our interpreter, that we could get food and rest less than two miles away. He also said there was a Trading Post within walking distance.

The young man said it was too bad we did not speak any English. It was something we had better learn if we wanted to stay in this New World. I nodded and smiled a lot, even though I did not understand the words so much.

The last thing I saw was the sun shining off of his gold tooth as he went up the ramp and disappeared below the deck of the trawler.

Now, at last, I knew what we had to do to get to this place called New York. But first, I will have to explain to Julianna how I fell and got my clothes so dirty in such a short time. I have never lied to her before.

Well…today may have to be my first time.

CHAPTER 13

"Where are you, America?"

MARRI:

This is the first thing I want to tell you today; I have been praying I will grow into a 'Beautiful Lady' like the Statue of Liberty. I saw so many rough-looking men start to cry when they looked up at her in the harbor. I want a young man to look at me like that one day. It will make coming to America even more wonderful than my wildest dream.

*****

Mama told us that we all had to sit on the edge of the two beds and wait for Papa before we could go up the stairs to see the United States. Mama sat on the bigger bed with Pauley and I had my arm around Lizzie. We were in the dark side of the room, sitting on the smaller bed.

All of a sudden, we heard booming footsteps coming down into the trawler. America at Last! My heart jumped and I yelled Papa's name! Lizzie was so happy she let out a great big scream. We all looked toward the dirty stairs...but it was not Papa that we saw.

Three members of the crew came down the steps, very deliberately. One man sat down next to Lizzie, another on Pauley's bed, and the third man sat near me. The man that could speak a little Hungarian smiled at Mama and told her we had to be searched before we could go across the ramp into the new country. The interpreter told us we needed to be free of any bad sickness or sores; things like that.

We let them feel our bodies all over. Mama did not like how

they did it to her, but Lizzie thought it was fun when one of the men tickled her. Pauley did not like it when they felt him under his shirt and pants. They even took off our shoes and looked at them, too. They felt our stockings; why, I'll never know. Our feet were not very clean, though.

I tried to look real pretty in my green dress with the blue flowers on it. Mama said she made it for me so I would look pretty as any of the young girls in New York City. The younger man loosened the belt on my dress, and felt under my grey slip. I thought he might be mad that I did not have a pretty white one.

Finally, the three men stood up, and the leader motioned toward our boxes and valises. He said, through the interpreter, that they have to search all of our belongings before we were allowed to take them up on deck.

I did not know what they were looking for, but for some reason, none of the men were smiling or being nice now...not even to Lizzie. She sat sobbing in the corner near a pile of dirty fish-net. I went and sat down next to her.

I did not know what to do, so I told her the men were playing a game of Hide and Seek. They were trying to tickle us, and make us laugh, so we would tell them a secret. Lizzie stopped crying. Mama looked over at me, and nodded her head up and down. That was her way of saying I did a good thing. I felt better, too.

The men finished going through all of our belongings. They found nothing they were looking for I guess, because of the very sad faces they all had. One of the men closed up the cases and taped each one shut with wide bands of a silvery-colored sticky tape. When he got through with each piece of our cases and other belongings, the other two men carried the things up the stairs to the deck. Finally, the last man went up the stairs.

We were alone at last. It was deathly quiet. I heard a fly buzzing around my head. It landed on Lizzie's nose. She shooed it away with her stuffed rag doll. At this moment, I felt I could close my eyes and fall asleep for a whole week.

*****

As I sat there with my arms around Lizzie, I started to think about the book. I hid it under the bottom step going up to the deck. I did not tell Mama or Papa that I picked up...actually, I stole it...a small crinkled paper book from the fancy building on Ellis Island while we were standing in line. I found it in the dirty room where Mama took us when Lizzie had to go to the bathroom. I hid the book because I did not want anyone to take it. I wanted to learn how to talk like an America girl. I can say some easy words. I am learning one new word...every day!

In the book are a lot of our own Hungarian words like 'stop' and 'go'; words like coffee, bread, and dozens of other words...all with a word next to it.

I've been learning the words, so Mama and Papa will be able to speak to these new people. All Papa knows how to say is 'NO'. You can not get very far in a new country with only one word. I am putting a circle around every word I have learned so far. 'KAVE' in Hungarian means 'COFFEE' in America. I think it means the same thing in Canada, the land we are in right now. I do not think Mama even knows where we are. Canada is North of the United States. I did not want to tell Mama, but we are a long way from Uncle Tobias.

*****

Mama was sitting in a chair close to the stairs. The boss of the three men, the interpreter, yelled from above. He told her she could now come up on deck and see Papa. She got up quickly and nodded her head, then hurried up the rickety steps.

I was so happy to see Mama smile for a change; now all of us would be able to see this new land...very soon!

*****

I heard Mama scream when she got to the top of the stairs! I could hear Papa trying to calm her down with soft, soothing

53

words in Hungarian. Pauley, Lizzie and I looked at each other. I was surprised that neither one started to cry.

This adventure was making my sister and brother so strong, they could never be hurt again; that is the way I felt at this very moment.

Mama shouted down at the three of us. Now it was our turn to wait until we were called. Lizzie looked like a statue sitting on the edge of the bed.

I grabbed my sister's and brother's hand and whispered a silent prayer for our parents. Then I told Lizzie and Pauley to stay on the big bed. I went over by the stairs and took my crinkled word book from under the bottom step and hid it in my bloomers. The man with the gold tooth will never think of looking for it there…I hope.

CHAPTER 14

"I can help, Papa!"

PAULEY:

I put my arms around Marri. I know people as old as Papa...
maybe young boys, even...are not supposed to cry. I could not
help it. I had watched as the men went through all of our things.
The interpreter told us they were checking our skin for big red
marks or bad scratches that would keep us out of the new country.
I did not believe them. They were looking for something else. I
knew they were looking for Papa's money.

Yes...I am only ten years old, but Papa had to tell one of us
where he was going to hide the money that Uncle Tobias sent him;
money that Papa and Mama would need to get us to New York City.
Papa told me to keep the secret...no matter how hard anyone tried
to get it from me.

*****

I was glad the men did not try to hurt me. I do not know what I
would have done. I know I am not as strong as Papa to keep a secret;
that is why I sat down next to Marri and hugged her. I knew she
would put her arms around me. That helped right away. I stopped
shaking.

We could hear Papa and Mama talking to each other on the
deck near the stairway. We could not make out the words, but at
least Mama was not yelling or crying anymore.

I looked across the room. Lizzie was sitting on the small bed
now. She had pulled the blanket on top of her head and put her
fingers in her ears. Lizzie did not want to hear what was going on.

She was humming a Cszardas; one of Papa's favorite songs. For some reason, that made me feel better, too.

All of a sudden, everything was so quiet. I could hear Marri breathing next to me. There were no sounds coming from the deck. I looked at my sister.

What was happening?

*****

Papa came down the first four steps from the deck. He leaned in and said we could all come up now. Marri and I stood up real quick. She wiped a dirty tear from my eye and smiled. Lizzie threw the blanket off her head and ran toward us. She had a beautiful smile on her face...her eyes dancing. This was the moment! We have been waiting for this special time for weeks and weeks!

Marri took Lizzie's hand and started up the steps. She was so excited, but I told her I wanted to be the last one to come up on deck. She looked at me, and I knew it would be okay with her. I took each step up very slowly. I felt that was the way Papa would have wanted me to do it.

Now...I was... almost...a young man.

*****

When I reached the deck, I saw that the sun would be setting very soon. It would be dark in less than two hours. Where will we be by then? I knew better than to worry about a simple thing like that. I was sure Papa knew where to go...and how to get there. Even Mama had a faint smile on her face.

We all hugged each other, then Mama and Papa picked up the two suitcases. Lizzie helped me and my sister carry the rest of our belongings down the ramp. At long last! My feet were on solid ground. Well...maybe not so solid; the yellow clay was kind of mushy.

Near the shoreline, I saw a giant white sign with dirty black letters on it. The sign read 'CANADA', and in smaller letters, the word 'WELCOME'. I could not read the sign, but Papa told us what it meant. He said this country was not too far from the United States...maybe two or three days. I was so happy to hear that. I knew Papa could lead us to this wonderful place called United States of America. In case you did not know it, those are the only words I know how to say in this new place.

Papa grabbed Lizzie and swung her up on his shoulders. She held her stuffed doll and a small cloth bag in one hand. Lizzie wrapped her other arm real tight around Papa's neck. With his free hand, he reached out for Mama's arm. She was carrying the smaller valise and a hand-made leather case.

I found out Papa had learned a new word from Marri; He said the word 'GO'. Then he turned and began walking South. At least we did not have to face that burning orange sun to our right. It would be almost dark in about a half hour.

Papa had a hold of Mama's arm so she would not fall in the bumpy road. Marri carried two small cardboard boxes. She was walking in front of me.

Papa said I could be a man today; he let me march in the back to pick up anything that was dropped. I felt older than ten. I was a Cossack today...without a horse!

CHAPTER 15

"My butt is sore!"

LIZZIE:

I was thinking about how nice it was when I was small...smaller than I am now. I held on to Mama's or G'Mama's hand as we walked around our vegetable garden in Dombrad. The flowers Mama planted around the edges along the fence were so pretty; lots of white and yellow daisies, pink and purple violets, and all the colored wildflowers I could ever imagine. G'Mama let us pick any flowers we wanted. She even let us take them up to the house and put them into our bedroom. I do not see any flowers in this country yet.

Pauley liked to climb our apple trees and toss down some of the big red apples. None of us kids liked to eat the green or yellow apples. The cherry trees were another of our favorites, too. If we were looking for Pauley, most of the time we could find him in the garden. I do not see any cherry or apple trees sitting from up here on Papa's shoulders.

*****

Before Papa put me up here, we watched while the man with the gold tooth and his workers walked back over the wooden bridge and onto their boat. They turned a big crank and a fat rope lifted the ramp from our side of the bank. The men tried to hold on to it, but it hit the deck of the boat with a great big bang! All of us watched the men finally tie the ramp into place near the rail of the old trawler.

We heard the engines start up. Some black smoke came out of

the boat near the top. Pretty soon it disappeared. The boat started to pull away from the rotted wooden dock. In just a few minutes, the trawler was in the middle of the small river. It turned away from the sun. We all watched until it went behind some trees...out of our sight forever.

Then Papa put me on his shoulders and said we are going for a walk. He said we will be going South on this dusty road that started from the edge of the river. I did not care which way we were heading. This was going to be lots and lots of fun!

******

Did I say fun?

Papa started marching along the yellow road. The pretty meadows were on both sides of us. In the distance, to our right, we could see a lot of blue water. We were going toward some giant trees about a half mile away. That is how far Papa said they were. I did not know how far that was; I was having a real good time on Papa's shoulders. Every step Papa took, we were getting nearer and nearer to the big trees.

Papa walked almost like the Cossacks did in our little town of Dombrad. He was humming a Hungarian song, and trying to keep up with the fast beat.

Pauley said he saw some big black birds flying in and out of the woods. I saw him picking up some small stones as we walked. He took a dirty handkerchief out of his pocket and tried to throw a stone with it. He was doing a pretty good job. He yelled at Papa to hurry; he wanted to get closer so he could hit the crows with a stone. Mama told him to be quiet.

I could tell that as we walked and walked, pretty soon Papa began to slow down...then slower...and slower. Then Mama said it was time for her to rest a while. Papa took me off his shoulders and told Mama that if she wanted to rest, it was all right with him.

*****

We rested, sitting on two big rocks, under a big tree that had lots of little white flowers. Pauley was going to climb it, but Mama said 'no'. She did not want him to fall and get hurt; Papa needed all of us to carry our things.

I lay on the ground, stretching my legs and rubbing my neck. Papa was doing the same. I could see that he needed the rest more than any of us. He just wanted to show us that he was still as strong as when he was a younger man. We all knew that.

The soft meadow felt good under my head, even though it was for just a little while.

I did not know how tired I was; I fell asleep right away.

*****

For the last eight months, Mama and Papa have been talking about coming to America. They kept saying it was 'The land of the Free'. None of us knew what that meant. We thought all of us were happy in Hungary.

Mama was always saying she wanted me and Marri to get married to a nice young man from America. She wanted all of her children to get a good education…whatever that meant.

She said all the people who live in America have lots of money, a big house, and even more than two horses! They have lots of land to grow crops and none of them ever have to worry about food. I did not understand what Mama meant; we never were hungry in Dombrad. Maybe older people need more food. I think that might be true.

Our town of Dombrad was very small. My parents knew almost everyone, even the people who lived on the hill. They were the most important ones in our little village. Papa always told us they would keep us safe from the Russians and even the Germans. If that was true, how come we had to leave Dombrad, and all my little friends, and travel half way around the world, looking for Uncle Tobias?

Oh…in case you do not know, I have never seen Uncle Tobias in my whole life.

*****

I was back again on Papa's shoulders. We were nearing what looked like a big forest. The trees were thick on both sides of the road. In the distance to our right, between some trees, we saw a giant mountain that had some snow on its top. Pauley wanted to hurry so we could play on it later today. Papa said 'no'. First, we had to find the United States.

Half way through the forest, we saw our first house near the bend in the road. It was set behind a clearing. Ruts in the dirt showed that whoever lived there had a wagon…and horses. I heard Papa tell Mama that we needed to find both of those things before we could go to see Uncle Tobias. Papa said it might be one or two days more before we see America.

I do not know about Pauley; my butt was getting sore.

CHAPTER 16

"The house in the woods."

JULIANNA:

I remember how our old farm in Dombrad looked on a beautiful Spring day like this one. When I close my eyes, I can still see the pale grey siding of our house and the two-piece door with the big black bolts. I could see the light brown and pink stones of the chimney. Benjamin and Gran'Papa carried all those stones from behind the creek, and laid them with loving care. The house was meant to last forever. The stones, I am sure, are still there; the house was burned to the ground before we left our beautiful village of Dombrad.

*****

I did not want to tell my Benjamin, but I was getting very tired. It was easy walking on our land in Europe, but this ground is filled with many holes. In some of the places, the holes have water in them; I think it comes from the mountains that are on both sides of us now. The sun was glistening off the top of the smaller one. Maybe we could learn to love this land, but I think it will take a long, long time.

Marri started to jump up and down; she was so excited! We could see a small creek leading up to the old house to our left. The dirt road we have been following divided into two roads near a big oak tree. A small shed, with the door off its hinges, was next to a barn. As we got closer, we could see one of the barn doors lying in the tall weeds, the other door leaning against the fence. Lizzie got off of Benjamin's shoulders and ran ahead with Marri. Pauley wanted to go with them, so I told him he could. He ran after the girls, waving his hat and yelling.

*****

Last year, as I tossed and turned on our mattress stuffed with hay, I dreamed of the day we would be welcomed by Uncle Tobias. He had written a long letter, telling us how we were to go through the big building on Ellis Island. Uncle Tobias said it only took them about six hours to be taken from the Island to the shores of this marvelous city called New York. Of course, his children did not cough like Lizzie.

All of us in our little town were so anxious to see the streets in this new world. In my dreams I could see it! Everyone told us that the streets in America were paved with gold! I wanted so much to see them for myself.

*****

The children were so excited! They honestly thought we might find Uncle Tobias waiting for us inside. Benjamin and I hurried up the winding yellow road that led to a small covered porch. Pauley was already climbing up one of the wooden posts that held up a low railing. It was made of short pieces of pine.

I put the small valise on the porch next to the door. The small box I had been carrying, I placed on top of Benjamin's suitcase. Pauley had set his two cartons near the door, close to the corner of the house. Benjamin picked up a piece of wood near the steps. He began to scrape some of the mud off his shoes. The children started to scream, pointing and laughing at their father. They wanted to see Uncle Tobias now!

Benjamin threw the stick away and knocked on the door.

CHAPTER 17

"I remember…"

BENJAMIN:

I remember how green the fields were at this time of the year on our land in Dombrad. I looked across the meadow as my family ran ahead of me to the house made of logs. This land was mostly for animals of the forest; not for farmers like me.

The sky did not seem as blue to me, either. Perhaps I was feeling just a little bit sorry that we left our homeland.

As I came near the house, I saw how crudely it was constructed. In Europe, we took the time to take the bark off the logs. On this house, much of the bark was hanging on the logs, with dirty green moss growing in the cracks. Dried mud was holding the house together. This was not a welcome sight for our family.

*****

I knocked on the door again; this time a little harder. The bottom rubbed the warped gray floorboards as I pushed in on the door, very carefully. It creaked for a moment. Pauley bumped the door with his shoulder and it finally opened.

We saw right away that the old house was empty. Julianna and the girls followed us inside. I told Pauley to make sure the rickety door was closed and barred. He liked it when I trusted him to do a hard job.

We stood in the middle of the large room. On the left side were some stairs, leading up to a loft that covered part of the ceiling. Under the loft there was a large wooden bed and a small table with an oil lamp on it.

To my right there was a sink, with running water from a hand pump. A small pile of wood was next to a dirty iron stove. The house had only three windows--one of them broken.

Julianna and Pauley pointed out the boards that were cut into the floor. I raised the hinged panel. We saw the stairway that led down to the sandy cellar.

I lit the tall candle on the sink and put it carefully in Marri's hands. She and Pauley went down the stone steps.

Pauley yelled up to us. He found some potatoes and was so excited! He ran up the stairs with three of them in his hands. Marri said she saw carrots and some green things; she was not sure what they were.

Julianna went down the steps to help the children. I heard her saying a special prayer for all of us.

Lizzie and I put some wood in the stove and made a fire. There was a lot of rain water in a bucket outside. We started to boil the water for cooking. Julianna made coffee that she found in an old cupboard. This was almost like home; now if we only had a cow.

*****

Julianna and Marri cooked the vegetables we found in the cellar. We all sat around the big wooden table in the center of the room, enjoying our first meal in a new country. We knew it was not the United States...but our family now had faith that soon we would be having supper in America!

Pauley said the potatoes were very good. I think he was trying to make his Mama feel better. Lizzie started to eat her potato. She wanted a special smile, too.

I mentioned to Julianna that Johan, the German interpreter from the trawler, told me there was a Trading Post perhaps a mile or two from this house. He said we could buy food and the things we will need to get to America.

Julianna wanted to know how we were going to buy supplies from the Trading Post if we did not have any money. I told her it was a store, where people could trade some of their possessions for the things they needed; like a horse and wagon.

The two of us began wondering what we had that the Trading Post would want. I decided it would be better to think about that tomorrow.

Julianna said the children could sleep in the loft tonight. Pauley was so excited. He started to run up the stairs, but she told him he had to wash his hands and face first.

The girls finished helping her clean off the table. Marri washed Lizzie's hands and face and they all hurried up the steps. My Julianna went to help them say their prayers.

*****

Julianna had thrown the potato peelings in a small bucket that was next to the stove. On top of it, I threw the rotted pieces of the vegetables we found in the cellar. I washed off the wooden top next to the rusty sink and carried it outside. I emptied the can and put it on the porch. This gave me a few minutes to walk around outside.

A four-foot high wooden fence was attached to the back of the house. I saw no animals of any kind. The fence ended about twenty feet to the East. It was nailed to the side of a small barn. The moon was shining through the trees; the barn looked empty to me.

My legs were aching. I was so tired, but I wanted to see what, if anything, I could find near the curved road.

I limped to the back of the house. I could see the outline of something made of wood in the tall weeds. Suddenly, the ache in my legs was gone! I hurried toward the shadowy form.

I saw the broken seat of a ten-foot long wagon. One of the smaller front wheels was missing, too. Maybe the wheel was in the barn! I got so excited! Perhaps I might find some other parts. I knew it could be repaired. Pauley and I could do it!

I took a long deep breath.

I would have to wait until morning to examine the rest of the wagon...and search the barn and grounds again.

It was too dark now.

I took another, deeper, breath and went inside.

*****

I felt I could have slept for two days, but I had a sacred duty to care for my family. No time for sleeping now.

I spread the map I had made during the last few days on the table, comparing it with the one I was given by the man with the gold tooth. Even the interpreter said the maps in this part of Canada are not very good. Perhaps the people at the Trading Post could mark the map and show us the best way to New York. It is only three days away. Isn't it?

*****

Dozens of things were going through my mind. I even thought I heard noises on the porch. I was so tired. So tired...

I closed my eyes for what I thought was just a moment.

Julianna shook my arm. I was still sitting at the table. She smiled down at me and said the children have been asleep now for almost an hour. I should come to bed. It was almost midnight.

I squeezed Julianna's hand. She looked at me and just nodded. That is all she needed to do. We were safe now...at least for one more day.

CHAPTER 18

"I can be funny, too!"

MARRI:

I was the first one of the children to wake up. Mama and Papa were downstairs, trying to be quiet, but I could hear Mama making something on the stove. They wanted us to have a good rest before we had to walk all the way to the Trading Post.

Lizzie was curled up in the corner of the bed, her head half covered by the dirty blanket. Pauley's arm was hanging over the side. He was still fast asleep at the foot of the small iron cot.

I washed my face in a pan of water we brought upstairs last night. We had it on a small table near the chimney. As I was wiping my face with a dirty grey towel, I looked out the window and saw the low dark clouds to the Northeast. It was going to rain today. I know that is what Papa will say when we sit down for breakfast. I wonder what we will have to eat; I hope it will not be more potatoes.

*****

Last night, Papa was telling us about the Trading Post. He said we could trade something we did not want. That way we could buy the things we needed—like maybe a horse.

When I heard Papa's words, I began to laugh. Papa was so serious. Everyone looked at me.

I said we could trade Pauley for lots and lots of food. Papa tried to wipe the smile from his face. Then I said we need a horse-- more than we need Pauley!

Lizzie did not like the idea. She said we should keep our only brother. Mama smiled at all of us and said we will get our horse without selling Pauley. Papa knew I was only trying to be funny. Papa was always so serious. I wondered why he had to be that way.

*****

Mama opened the door to the loft. She took two steps up the rickety stairway and called our names. First, she yelled my name. Mama's voice sounded so happy this morning. I was not even a bit surprised. She called Pauley and Lizzie's names next. I still had to go over and give them both a little shake before they sat up in bed. Pauley said he wanted to go back to sleep.

Pauley was more tired than little sister. He tried to be like Papa all day yesterday…and now he was so tired; he was almost as tired as Papa.

I heard Mama and Papa talking in the kitchen. Their voices carried all the way up to the loft. Papa sounded like he had a very good sleep, too. He sounded like a new man. For a moment, I wondered why.

All of a sudden, I knew the answer.

I heard another voice in the room; a familiar voice. Yet I could not remember who it was. Then I heard the slight German accent trying to speak our Hungarian language.

OH, MY! I know who it is!

I threw my clothes on as fast as I could. I ran down the stairs and pushed the door open.

There he was…sitting at the table!

CHAPTER 19

"Can I ride the horse?"

PAULEY:

I ran down the stairs behind Marri. Mama told me to be careful and not push my sisters. Papa walked over by the steps and said he had a surprise for us all.

When I saw Johan, I did not know what to say. He looked at me and shook my hand, as if I was a long-lost relative. He even hugged Lizzie and Marri. I did not know he liked us so much. Maybe I am too young to understand older people.

Mama and Papa were smiling, drinking their coffee with our 'new' friend. I do not know where Mama got the coffee, but she was always very good at making things out of nothing.

On the corner of the table, I saw the old map that Papa has been carrying and marking on while we were on the trawler. He always sharpened his pencil with the ivory-handled knife he carried in his vest pocket. I watched as Johan told him where to mark an 'X' on the map. Papa did it very carefully. Johan said that was now the exact spot where our family was standing. He also said we were a long, long way from New York. I turned and saw the very sad look on Mama's face.

*****

Listening to Johan reminded me of my German friends, Karl and Henry. I met them on the ship that was bringing us to America, remember? We had so much fun playing and running around the deck and especially down in the Steerage Section. It seemed like such a long time since I saw them. Papa is keeping a log of our travels. He said it has been only six days ago.

*****

Johan told us that he tried to get in the house early this morning, but the door was bolted. He said the window was nailed shut so he slept in the barn, covering himself with some of the yellowish-colored hay.

I heard him tell Papa that he would lead us to the Trading Post. It was not where the man with the gold tooth said it was. The Trading Post is not South; it is Southeast—about a four-hour journey. Johan said it was a short trip, if you had a horse. If we would have hiked directly to the South, we would have gone toward the lake. At that point, there are no means of crossing into the United States.

Johan said we could go across the lake from Canada, to Pennsylvania or Michigan. These were just words to me, and I think also to Papa and Mama. He said it could be only another four days or so before we would be in America.

When I heard that word, America, I could see Mama and Papa's eyes get real big. We all knew now that it was only a matter of time…before we saw our Uncle Tobias.

I heard Papa and Johan talking about horses. I got really excited! I asked Papa if we could buy a horse at the Trading Post. Then we could bring it back here to this house. Mama and the girls would not have to walk anymore. Papa said I was starting to sound like a grown man. He said I was old enough to help us get to America. He would buy the horse for me.

Papa thanked Johan for being so nice to us. He looked at me and said I could call him 'Uncle' Johan.

What I would really like to know is why Johan came back to help Papa.

CHAPTER 20

"It is my turn-- now!"

<u>LIZZIE:</u>

I ran across the wooden bridge that led to the barn. Mama did not want me to go with the men, but I begged her until she said 'GO'. That was the first time I heard Mama say a word in another language. It sounded so funny.

My nice Uncle Johan picked me up and threw me in the air! I flew with my arms spread out—just like an eagle! Papa never did that to me. Maybe I could learn to like Uncle Johan.

He also said they would rather take me to the Trading Post, but Papa already told Pauley he could go and ride a horse. I guess that was the best thing to do. I did not really want to go.

*****

I watched while Papa and our new friend searched every corner of the barn. They climbed a tall ladder that went up to a hayloft too, but the only thing they found there were some dead birds and a bent pitchfork.

The four of us searched all around the outside of the barn, and behind the small woodshed. We found a broken plow. Pauley dug up some old rusty horseshoes.

Uncle Johan said they should go to the Trading Post as soon as Mama packed a small basket of food and some water. He knew Mama and us girls would be safe while they were gone. Papa said they better leave now, so they could be back before dark. Uncle Johan nodded.

The three of us hurried up to the house to tell Mama.

*****

My job was to sit at the corner window and watch for Papa. The sun was almost hidden by the tall birch trees.

I got up from the chair about an hour later and knelt on the pillow, so I could stretch and maybe see better. That was when Mama told me it was time to go outside. I ran as fast as I could to the bend in the road. She said Marri could come out to watch with me, as soon as she finished peeling the potatoes.

I was watching for Papa, Uncle Johan, and Pauley to come back from the Trading Post. I sat down by the yellow dirt road, past the giant Maple tree. I waited for almost an hour. It would be dark soon.

There is Pauley! Riding a horse—without a saddle!

I saw my brother on the horse, dragging a wagon wheel that was tied with rope to some wooden planks. It looked like he was pulling a crudely-made sled. On the wagon wheel was a big cardboard box. It was tied to the top with baling wire.

Pauley looked so happy! He had been looking forward to riding a horse since we left our native land. I saw something else! He was wearing a pair of dirty black leather boots, almost like the Cossacks wore in Dombrad.

Pauley waved at me, hanging on to the reins with his other hand. I could see Marri as she came running from the house, too. Pauley stopped the horse in the middle of the road. He told us that Papa and Uncle Johan were coming behind him. They are not too far away, on the other side of that big hill. He pointed toward some gray clouds low on the horizon.

Oh…one more thing. Pauley said Papa bought a shotgun at the Trading Post. Uncle Johan told him to buy it.

I ran back to the house and yelled 'Papa's Home!'

CHAPTER 21

"The memories keep coming back."

JULIANNA:

Sometimes I wake up in the middle of the night. I still see the children's Gran'Papa falling on our porch, with the bullets in his chest. I see our house being emptied of all our possessions. I see the barn in my dreams too, with the soldiers taking the animals and then setting fire to the hayloft. But most of all, I still see the dead bodies in the ditches. Men, women and children, and even some soldiers, sprawled at the sides of the road. We were leaving our little village because of the war. Our country just happened to be in the middle of all the killings.

We wanted to go to a land of freedom. Perhaps it was just a few miles away. We kept walking with our children and our meager belongings.

When we reached the next village, and saw more devastation and more dead bodies, Benjamin and I knew we had to leave our once proud country, Hungary, forever.

*****

I heard Lizzie screaming. Marri ran back toward the house. She yelled for me to come outside. Right Now!

I took the big heavy pot of potatoes off of the stove and carried it to the stone counter by the sink. I wiped my hands in a grey towel and hurried outside. I could not believe my eyes!

Pauley was sitting on a horse. He did not have a saddle, only a huge smile on his face. He waved at me as I ran down the dirt road. Marri was holding the horse's reins and patting its mane. It was an old plow horse, but Pauley did not mind; he was happy to be riding bareback.

He told us Benjamin and Uncle Johan are about a half-mile behind him. We would see them coming around the bend in the road very soon.

Pauley showed me the used boots that the man at the Trading Post gave him as a present for being such a help to his father. Marri opened the top of the large wooden box and took out a bag of shotgun shells, some bacon, and two loaves of bread. Pauley said Papa was bringing two chickens for me to cook for tonight's dinner.

Marri said Pauley saw their first farmer at the Trading Post, but the farmer had a funny hat; it was made of cowhide, not straw like in our town.

Pauley jumped off the horse and said the man in charge of the Trading Post let him ride a pony from their corral. It was almost like riding his pony in Dombrad. Pauley said he could grow to like it in this country, if there were more people like the man at the Trading Post...and he did not even know his name.

There they are! Thank you, God! It will be dark soon!

Benjamin and Johan were now past the bend in the road. They both waved at us and shouted our names. It was so good to see them again.

I could see the long shotgun. Johan was holding it with one hand, the barrel of the gun resting on his shoulder. The girls started to run toward their father.

It was then that I noticed the chickens. Benjamin had them tied at their necks with a heavy twine. He was pulling them along as if he was walking two dogs. When they came closer, I began to laugh. The chickens began to cluck louder; I think they knew what was in store for them.

CHAPTER 22

"I love them so."

BENJAMIN:

We could see Pauley as he rounded the bend in the road. He passed the trees on the right side of the lane that led to the old house. Johan and I watched him until he disappeared.

Our Uncle Johan was walking ahead of me about ten yards or so. He carried the shotgun, cradling it since we left the Trading Post. He said there might be a pheasant or a squirrel hiding somewhere in the brush; he wanted to be ready to give the children something to eat—besides potatoes.

In Europe, the fields are less traveled. Near Dombrad, we would have seen dozens of birds by now. Johan finally put the shotgun over his shoulder.

Watching Johan as we plodded along the road reminded me of the fitful dream I had last night. It has been bothering me since I woke up this morning. I still cannot understand why I could dream such a strange, and disturbing, dream about Johan.

*****

I woke up in a sweat. Why, I did not know.

As always, every morning, I reach under the bed for my hat. It was not there! Only Mama knows that I have Uncle Tobias' address sewn in my hat, along with the rest of the American money he sent us. I had gone into the bathroom at the Trading Post to take some of it out of the lining to pay for the horse and wagon wheel. I used some to pay for the chickens and the food. I did not think Johan saw me do it. Did he see me take out the stitches in the hatband and sew it up again?

In my dream, I saw Johan smiling at me. He had a strange twinkle in his eyes. He had his arms folded across his chest. His coat pocket had a big handkerchief hanging out of it. I wondered if that was our money. Maybe I could wait until Johan went to sleep. I could take the money back from his pocket. Maybe I could...

Is that why Johan came back? I woke up in a sweat.

*****

Johan called my name. I was not so sure if it was still a dream or not. He shouted 'Benjamin' again, this time a little louder. He said Marri and Lizzie were running toward us, waving their arms and yelling Papa! Papa!

Johan pointed at the girls as they took a shortcut and ran off the road into the grassy fields. Two pheasants flew into the air. We were all so excited; we did not even try to shoot them. A rabbit ran out of the brush. We all ignored it, too.

Johan said he and Pauley could fix the wagon while I returned to the Trading Post. He reminded me that I would have to go back and repair some boots and work shoes for several people. This would give me a chance to earn a few extra dollars before we went on the Ferry later this week.

The girls gave both of us a big hug. I saw Julianna, standing next to Pauley. She had the most beautiful smile on her face. I was so happy to see my family again.

I hugged Julianna...the first time since we left Dombrad.

She kissed me, burying her face in my beard. At that moment, we knew our life in America was going to be wonderful.

Just to be on the safe side, I believe I will sleep with the shotgun near my bed tonight.

CHAPTER 23

"Follow the yellow dirt road!"

MARRI:

My best friend in Dombrad was Ilonka. She was three years older than me. I tried to be like her. She was beautiful and had coal-black hair. She was a wonderful dancer, too.

I think 'Ilonka' in English is 'Helen'. I have heard that everyone in America likes to shorten their name. When she comes here, we could call her 'Hel'. I have been dreaming about her every day since we left Hungary. I do not know why.

*****

I gave Papa a big hug, too…right after Mama kissed him on his hairy face. Oh, my! They must really love each other!

Pauley showed me the blanket he was sitting on while he rode the horse all the way from the Trading Post. He said it was a lot of fun…only now, he said his butt was sore.

I just heard Uncle Johan tell Papa that it will be a little over a half-day's ride on a Ferry and a Barge to cross the big lake to go to a place called Pennsylvania. It is in America. We will be seeing Uncle Tobias soon! Thank God!

Papa said he will help Pauley and Uncle Johan fix the big wooden wheel for the old wagon. They wanted to work on it in the barn after supper. Uncle Johan stood up and told Papa to go and rest for a while; he and Pauley can fix it.

Tomorrow, when Papa goes to the Trading Post to repair some shoes and boots, Pauley is going to fix the broken reins while Johan puts the wheel on the wagon. Uncle Johan said he will show Pauley how to heat the old horseshoes they found in the barn, and reshape them to fit the horse's hoofs. Pauley got so excited; he wanted to start working with Uncle Johan before he ate his supper.

Later, I asked Papa what a 'Ferry' and a 'Barge' was. He said he did not know. Papa told me to ask Uncle Johan because he could tell me anything I wanted to know about this land and all the strange things in it.

Uncle Johan said he was from Germany, but he has been traveling around America for years; he helps people find their relatives in this new land. At least that is what he told me.

Oh, oh! I hear Mama calling me. She wants me to go and help her peel some more potatoes for supper. When I grow up, I will never eat another potato as long as I live!

I never got a chance to ask Uncle Johan what a 'Ferry' and a 'Barge' was.

I ran into the house when Mama called my name for the second time. We knew what would happen if she had to call our names once more; no potato pancakes for supper!

Hum...maybe that would not be so bad tonight!

CHAPTER 24

"Look! I am a Cossack!"

PAULEY:

I was leading the parade, riding my favorite horse down the middle of our little town in Dombrad. All the girls were watching me. I could see dozens of them standing at the sides of the road, waving and smiling at me. A cute young blonde-haired girl screamed and jumped up and down as I waved back at her.

The saddle was made of shiny black leather, matching the color of my horse. I had polished the silver trimmings around the stirrups and the fancy saddle. The lariat was white with flecks of silver. My big black hat…

*****

The screaming stopped. All I could hear was the shallow breathing coming from my sisters. We were sleeping in the loft above the wooden stairway. Marri was still fast asleep, but Lizzie was whimpering in her sleep like she often does.

I have been sleeping upstairs on a small mattress at the foot of their bed the last two nights, close to the stairs leading down to the kitchen. Papa said it was better for me to sleep up in the loft with the girls, in case they became frightened; he said they needed a man to protect them. I think he was trying to make me feel good. Papa just wanted to sleep with Mama without me always kicking them from the other side of the bed.

I opened my eyes and sat up, listening to the voices. I strained to hear Mama and Uncle Johan talking. At times they seemed to be whispering; I could barely hear what they were saying. Funny—I did not hear Papa's voice at all.

Uncle Johan and Mama were talking a little louder now. I could smell the bacon frying and the noise of some dishes being moved around. I heard the sounds of a chair as it was pulled across the wooden floor and Mama sitting down with a great big sigh. I could finally hear what they were both saying:

Papa had gotten up very early to go to the Trading Post and repair some shoes and boots. The owner said he would pay Papa for the repairs that would take most of the day. Papa was happy to do it, because he and Uncle Johan said we needed more money to get all the way to New York; this was a good way to get some. I was surprised to hear that Papa rode the horse to the Trading Post.

I ran down the stairs into the kitchen. Mama told me to be careful when I slipped on the last step. She gave me a big hug and a kiss on my cheeks. I was surprised when she did it.

Uncle Johan said he was going out to the barn to fix the wheel and the reins. He told me I could help him as soon as I had my breakfast.

*****

The wheel was easy to put on the wagon. We greased all the moving parts on the other wheels, too. It was fun.

Later, I helped Uncle Johan fix the reins. I held the black leather pieces while he made some new holes in it. The things that looked like nails kept falling out of the old holes. He said we need good reins for the horses so they would go where we wanted them to go. This was hard work; I did not like it.

While Johan was finishing the reins, he told me to clean the rust off of some old horseshoes we found in the barn. It was a hard job, but he patted me on the head for the good job I did. He said he will nail the shoes on the horse when Papa gets back from the Trading Post. He said we have two extra horseshoes to put in the wagon when we start our 4-day journey to the lake.

This was a big surprise to me. I did not know we were going

on a 4-day journey. Why is it? The smallest kid is always the last to know!

******

When we finished our jobs, late in the afternoon, I asked Uncle Johan if we could name the horse. He told me the only name that horses understand is 'Git-Up! I said KING would be a nice name. I even said 'please', which I hardly ever say. He finally looked at me and said it was okay to name the horse KING if I wanted. Uncle Johan said I was such a big help to him. If the horse having a name made me happy, he was happy.

While he was in such a good mood, I asked him if he had any money. How could he live without money—or not have his own horse and other stuff?

Uncle Johan stopped what he was doing and looked at me. He rubbed his chin. I saw his eyes turn several shades darker. I was truly amazed to see that. It was so strange.

Finally, in a very slow, serious tone, he said he helps people—and they pay him. It was as simple as that. He got up and said he had to go wash his hands.

I wondered if Papa paid Uncle Johan. And if he did, where does Papa keep his money. It is not in our suitcases. I know...because I looked there.

Marri opened the front door and beat on a pan with a big wooden spoon and yelled to us that supper was ready.

Potato pancakes...not again!

CHAPTER 25

"America—here I come!"

LIZZIE:

Very early this morning, while they thought we were all asleep, I heard Papa and Uncle Johan talking. They were sitting at the table drinking some of Mama's black coffee that she makes every night. The men like their coffee so you can stand a spoon in it. That is what Uncle Johan always tells me.

Papa was saying that he has to go back to the Trading Post for one more day. The owner liked the way he fixed the shoes and boots that had holes in them. Papa said the man gave him two dollars in some strange Canadian money for each one he made better. Some of the shoes belong to people called Miners and Lumber-Jacks. Those are funny names!

Uncle Johan thought it was best for him to go and do the work. He told Papa that we will need all the money that can be earned by the time we get to America.

I crawled out of bed and peeked down at the people from the top edge of the stairs. I saw Mama come into the kitchen. She had been outside, by the water pump, cleaning another pile of potatoes for tonight's supper. She was carrying the heavy pail across the room, past the woodpile near the front door. Uncle Johan got up from his chair, took the potatoes from her, and dumped them into the sink. I could tell Mama was surprised by the look on her face. I do not think Papa ever did something like that; cooking is women's work, he always said. Maybe in America, things will be different.

Uncle Johan said he had to go out to the barn and fix the seat on the front of the wagon. It would not take him long to do it; maybe three or four hours.

Before he went out the door, I heard him tell Papa to let us know about the long ride we will be taking on a 'Ferry' soon. I did not know what a 'Ferry' was; I do not think Mama knows, either. She went to the sink and began cleaning more potatoes.

Papa got up from his chair as soon as Uncle Johan went out the door. I peeked through the broken upstairs window. I saw Papa lead the horse from the barn and put a torn blanket on its back. Papa had to climb on the fence and swing his leg over the back of the horse. He passed the corner of the road just as the sun was coming up over the trees.

Papa never said a word to us about the 'Ferry'. I asked Mama if I could go to the barn and help Uncle Johan. She said it would be good for me to get out of the kitchen. I believe she wanted to be alone.

I was glad she told me to go; now I could ask Johan if he would tell me what a 'Ferry' is, and why we have to go on it.

I ran all the way to the barn. I talked to Uncle Johan for a long time. I even helped him pick up some nails. He told me all about the 'Ferry', and a thing called a 'Barge'. It is a floating Island that can take us to the United States! Oh, MY!

I hurried out of the barn. I wanted to be by myself...just like Mama. I closed my eyes and began to think of all the wonderful things we will have in America. Some day I will have my own house. Some day I will have my own children.

Tomorrow might be the day we go to America; Uncle Johan called it 'Pen-Cil-Vane-E-Ah'. That is the first American word I know how to say. I have so much to learn.

It is hard to be the youngest in the family. Most of the time, nobody pays attention to me. But I see all that is going on.

I did not want to tell Mama, but I started to cough again. I think the hay in the barn tickled my throat.

CHAPTER 26

"The next few days…"

JULIANNA:

I needed to be alone. The house was empty now except for Marri. She was up in the loft, looking for the book of words she was learning to speak. I told her to take all the time she needed; I wanted a few minutes of peace and quiet. This was the best time of the day for my prayers.

I prayed for my hard-working husband of twenty years and our three wonderful children. I prayed for people like Johan and the man at the Trading Post for taking their time to help us.

I thanked our God for his blessings and our new life in this strange land…America. I prayed, too, for these next few days. They may be some of the most important days of our lives as we try to find our Uncle Tobias in New York.

As I prayed, like always, I began to feel more relaxed and secure. Now I was ready to meet the day.

*****

I could hear the faint pounding sounds coming from the barn. Johan and Pauley were working hard to get the old wagon fixed. Johan told me this morning that the wagon will be finished before supper time. Bless him for helping us, God.

I was going to make a top for the wagon out of an old blanket. My little one, Lizzie, asked me what would happen if it rained on it and got all wet. She said the water would come through the blanket and get us all wet. She was right, of course.

Johan said Benjamin will be bringing a ten-foot canvas cover from the Trading Post later today. He says the wagon will be ready for us to travel in before the sun comes up. Bless him.

Benjamin says he will have to work at the Trading Post for another four days. Alex, the owner, likes Benjamin because every shoe he works on, Benjamin repairs it as if it was his own. He can make new boots, and logger's shoes, too. He can also make the old wore-out shoes look brand new.

Because of Benjamin's good works, Johan tells me that our family may have to be apart for a little while; perhaps a few days. I did not like to hear that. We have never been apart...not even in Dombrad. Do we need to have this money so badly?

Bright and early tomorrow, Johan wants to start on a four-day trip which will take us to a place called Shawnee Bay. It is on this side of the giant lake that takes us to America. Johan says that is where we are going to take the 'Ferry' that pulls the giant 'Barge'. He told me that the weather will be good for only one week; then the rains might come for two or three weeks. He explained to me that if we wanted to transport the wagon and horse, they would have to be loaded on this big floating island called a 'Barge'. This was the only way we would be able to get into the United States before the rainy season.

Benjamin has told me nothing about this 'Ferry' and 'Barge' business; he is more concerned with his tasks at the Trading Post. It will be hard for us to part, even for a few days.

Johan says Benjamin might be able to meet us on the other side of the lake, perhaps early next week, at a place called 'Jamie's Landing'—and it is in the United States! Thank God!

I do not know if this is such a good thing to do... but I am so thankful for a wonderful friend like Johan. I believe he is trying to do his best to help me, Benjamin and the children.

What reason would he have in not trying to help us?

I am going to pray about this, too—right now!

CHAPTER 27

"If I was a rich man…"

BENJAMIN:

I tried to learn how to play the violin when I was just a young boy. I was around twelve years old when my father bought me a used instrument from a local Gypsy.

No matter how much I practiced, I could never get my old violin to 'cry'. The only thing that was 'crying' was me. I had to shake the fingers on my left hand as I pushed on the strings, and at the same time, slowly pull the bow up and down with my right hand. The sounds from that violin were terrible.

The Gypsies made it look so easy. My father loved to sit down next to the violin player and sing along with the music. He would close his eyes as he sang; he was in another world. I wanted to make my father happy, too. I practiced for hours and hours, trying to do what they showed me, but the fingers on my left hand were always sore and bleeding.

A month later my violin teacher put his hand on my shoulder, shook his head as he looked down at me, and told me that I should take up shoemaking instead. He was right!

Perhaps I could sell you a good, slightly-used, violin?

*****

I was the best shoemaker in all of Dombrad. Everyone bought their shoes from me if they needed a new pair. The entire village also came to me for all of their shoe repairs, too; the men, women and children…it did not matter to me.

Humm…now, when I think about it…I was the one, and only, shoemaker in our beautiful little town.

******

Today is the beginning of my second week of work at the Trading Post. Every day I have noticed something different as I ride back and forth on Pauley's horse, King.

This 'Wonder' horse has only one way to travel—slow! When Pauley rides him, he can go at a gallop, like a happy colt. Then again, I may weigh four or five times as much as Pauley. If I was this old horse, perhaps I would do the same.

Now I understand. King may be slow, but he IS smart!

*****

I turned toward the Trading Post at the fork in the road. The sun was trying to fight its way through the tops of the red oak trees to my right. I could see it was going to be a beautiful Spring day… almost as beautiful as it would be in Dombrad.

*****

I have only been in this country called Canada for a short time, but I can tell this land is not good for farmers like me. The weather is too cold and raw. The fields always seem to be too wet from the rain waters coming from the lakes and down from the mountains. Perhaps that is why we do not see too many horses… mostly mules.

We see lots of mules at the Trading Post. The workers in Canada use them to pull big wagons loaded with trees. The trees have been cut down by men called 'Lumberjacks'. From what I can see in this short time, these trees are turned into lumber for new barns, stores, and other types of construction.

I have learned one other important thing; Canada's land is good for mining also. The miners work in the hills and mountainsides all throughout this area. That is why Alex needs me to work at the Trading Post. Most of the men I have met there work as Lumberjacks, hauling the trees to a mill further West, just this side of a place called Jamie's Landing.

Johan tells me that we will be able to send a letter to our Uncle Tobias once we get to this 'Landing' place. I still do not know how far it is from New York. Just by looking at my old scratched-up maps, it may be another two weeks of traveling in our make-shift wagon. I pray it would not be any longer.

*****

I have no desire to be a miner, or a lumberjack. Uncle Tobias says this America is made for the farmer. I can see what he says is the truth. That is why I came to this new land...and that is what I want to be.

*****

Once Alex found out I was a shoemaker, he told me I could work for him as long as I wanted. When he saw how beautifully I could repair the old shoes, he got an even better idea. He wanted me to teach two young men how to make and repair shoes for the Miners and the Lumberjacks.

That sounded like a good idea...at first. I thought I could earn enough money for us to get all the way to New York without Julianna having to worry so much. But then I said to Alex that I cannot make a shoemaker out of a young man in one week--not even in two months.

I reminded Alex that we wanted to go to America and live in New York close to our relatives. He knew in his heart that Canada did not have the good soil for real farmers like me.

The owner of the Trading Post finally said I could teach them for as long as I was in Canada. I agreed to those terms. We shook

91

hands. I started to repair the two dozen old shoes that were stacked in a corner of one of the stockrooms.

*****

Near the end of my work day, Alex called me into his small office. He introduced me to two men. He said they were very good friends of Johan; both had worked for him on the trawler a few months ago. Both of them had part-time jobs as mill-hands at the local lumber yard. I shook hands with Carl and his younger brother Kurt. They told me Johan gave them free passage on his trawler last year. Carl said they were from Germany. Their family did not like the fighting going on in Europe any more than we did. Now they wanted to go to the United States too, but they needed to earn money for their way on the Ferry. They looked like very nice young men.

Carl was two years older than his brother. He shook my hand vigorously and told me that Johan was their good friend, too. He said Johan will see to it that our family will get to America. Kurt just looked at me and smiled.

I have seen that same smile somewhere…lately.

*****

It was a very long day. The ride back to the old house seemed like it would never end. Lizzie was standing by the front door, yelling and waving at me. When she ran inside, I knew Julianna was getting my supper on the table.

Johan came out of the house. He took the reins from me and led the horse to the trough at the side of the barn. He said we could talk after I ate my chicken soup and potatoes.

Julianna knew I had something special to tell her. She was sitting across the table, waiting for me to finish my supper.

I was amazed at what she could do with these same old potatoes day after day. Perhaps they tasted so good because I knew we were getting closer and closer to our destination. I ate as quickly as I could.

The moment she saw me pick up my gray hat, Julianna was at my side.

*****

I told her that Alex would pay me $100.in American money. To get that large amount, I would have to teach Carl and his brother how to put the special nails in the bottoms of the leather boots used by the loggers. I would also have to teach them how to make repairs to the boots. This added work would take me perhaps another week…maybe longer. I was not sure.

I also told Julianna that Alex is letting me ride a horse that he has for sale at the Trading Post. I can ride it back and forth every day, but first I'll have to walk there early tomorrow to get it. Alex is supplying the saddle, blanket and reins.

I saw the tears in Julianna's eyes. She did not say a word. I touched her hand ever so gently, then told her I needed to talk to Johan. I wiped the dirty hatband with my grey handkerchief and went outside to find him.

*****

But first, I walked to the other side of the barn, near that old giant oak. Last week, I had dragged a small wooden crate I found next to the burned-out shed. I shoved some hay under the old blanket and made myself a comfortable seat on top of it.

I do not think anyone knows it is here. This is my own Special Place. Over the years, I have found that Prayer is the only way to find the answers to our problems. I had a wonderful teacher. Thank you, Julianna.

A few minutes later, when I turned around, I saw Johan watching me from behind the tree. He pulled his head back quickly. I am sure he did not want me to see him watching as I prayed about our search for freedom in America.

I needed to see him before he took my family to Shawnee Bay. I hurried to the tree. I thought I saw tears in his eyes as he came toward me.

We talked for only a few minutes. Johan sounded like he had a cold. I felt strange knowing that a grown man had seen me praying behind a big old oak.

Finally, we shook hands. I thanked him for all he has done for us. I told him we will meet again in one week at Shawnee Bay. Johan nodded. We did not know what else to say.

He turned and hurried back to the house.

*****

During the night, I had visions of thousands of pairs of shoes dancing across the lake. Then I saw horses flying over the water's edge, on their way to America. Julianna saw me tossing and turning and muttering in my sleep. She leaned over to my side of the bed and kissed me on the cheek. It was past midnight. I finally fell asleep.

CHAPTER 28

"I am thirsty already!"

<u>MARRI:</u>

Last night, I saw Papa praying in his special place. He always prays next to the big red tree behind the barn. Papa took his hat off, wiped the hatband, and little by little, as he prayed, he twisted and turned his hat, all the while looking at the tree. Maybe he sees God sitting up there, waiting to talk to him. I believe he does, because Papa is always smiling when he comes inside after praying. I think I will look around to find my own favorite place to pray.

*****

It was real late when we said a tearful goodbye to Papa. He hugged all of us before we went up to the loft. Papa told us that he would be gone to his work at the Trading Post before the sun came up in the morning. He said he will be there for at least one week—perhaps longer.

Lizzie started to cry even more when Papa told us we would not see him during that time because the rest of us will be traveling with Johan.

Papa told Pauley that the man at the Trading Post gave him some sugar for King. Papa said the horse will be working very hard, pulling the wagon and five people all the way to Shawnee Bay. Papa took the sugar out of the cupboard next to the sink and gave it to Pauley. I could see the tears in both of their eyes. Papa put a hand on Pauley's shoulder.

We all hugged Papa again. Mama gave him the biggest hug. I

saw Papa shake hands with Johan. He told him we will meet again at Shawnee Bay in one week, without fail!

*****

Mama woke me when it was still dark outside. She told us to get dressed before we went down to eat our breakfast. I hurried as fast as I could; she said we were having eggs this morning! I knew this was going to be a special day!

*****

I was the one who told Uncle Johan to tie a small barrel to the side of the wagon and fill it with water. I thought it was a real good idea. I think he did it just to please me. After the first mile, I could see lots of small creeks and water holes.

Johan followed the road that went a little bit to the left. He said it was the road that goes toward the lake, away from the Trading Post. I was surprised when I heard him tell Mama, that right now, we were still twenty miles away from Shawnee Bay. Johan told Mama it will take us four days to get there.

I began to wonder how many times he has helped other people get to this place on the lake called Shawnee Bay.

******

Uncle Johan told us that we were going to rest now. He said we had already gone two miles! My goodness! I am not even tired, but I can see Pauley and Lizzie are glad we stopped.

It will be a hot day. Johan told me it was good to bring the water. Sometimes, he said, the water we find tastes just like baby frogs! Ugh!

CHAPTER 29

"Boots and Berries—Oh, My!"

PAULEY:

I did not want to tell Mama that I was getting tired, but I was so glad when Uncle Johan said it was time to rest. I told him it was a good idea, because I knew my sisters and Mama needed to stop for a while. I said I was not even tired.

When Uncle Johan told us we had traveled now for only two miles, I was so surprised; it felt more like TEN miles!

Papa always tells me that I am almost a man. I cannot let my sisters see that they are stronger than me. I told Marri and Lizzie that Uncle Johan was stopping mostly because of them and Mama. They just looked at each other and smiled. I was not really sure what that meant.

I went to the side of the wagon and took a long cool drink, then sat down in the soft grass with my back against one of the wheels. I closed my eyes for only one second.

*****

I was riding my favorite white pony through the center of our little town. The parade was in celebration of Dombrad's Founder's Day. My new friend Maria, who will be coming to America someday, was smiling and waving her hands as I rode past. She ran after me, throwing red streamers, flowers and handfuls of rice. I waved back and blew her a kiss.

In this dream, I saw myself as a tall man, about twenty years old, with dark curly hair. I wore a tall black hat with white feathers on it. My uniform was black and white with fancy braid all over it and a bright red stripe down the side of my pants. I even had a curved sword in a scabbard hanging from the saddle.

I reached down and began rubbing my black shiny boots that came up to my knees. I do not know why, but it felt so good to rub them...so good...so...

*****

Uncle Johan woke me, shaking my arm. He wanted to know why I was rubbing my dirty black boots. He smiled at me as he said it. I wondered if I had been talking out loud.

Mama said I should eat my lettuce and potato sandwich before we get back on the wagon. She said everyone else had finished eating. It was time to get back on the wagon.

Uncle Johan says we will be traveling almost three more miles before we are going to stop for the night.

I put a little extra potato and a pickle in my sandwich.

*****

We were all riding in the wagon this morning. There were no trees or bushes of any kind. The land was perfectly flat as we traveled. But now, Uncle Johan said he had to turn the wagon South, toward the lake. Within a half-hour, our wagon was going back and forth between trees, large bushes, and across some small creeks. It was more fun, now!

Uncle Johan told me to get off the wagon and walk along the creek beds. He said I was the one with the nice boots, remember? My job now was to look for berries, or fruits of any kind, as we rode along. I jumped down and ran ahead of the wagon. This was getting to be even more fun!

CHAPTER 30

"A man with funny feathers!"

LIZZIE:

The land ahead looks like a giant sea of yellowish green grass. It reminds me about our ride on the ship. The ocean water looked just like this. It is so beautiful. I am beginning to love America more and more every day.

I started to get sleepy too, just like Pauley did this morning, but our wagon was so bumpy. I could not fall asleep.

I sat up in the back of the wagon behind Uncle Johan. He was steering the horsey. I rubbed one of my knees against a dirty gray board and my long brown stocking got a big hole in it. I'll ask Marri to sew it later when we stop for the night. Mama gave them to me before we left Dombrad. I do not want her to see that I was not being careful.

I hope it does not rain, because the top of the wagon has lots of small holes in it. Uncle Johan did not have time to patch them; he said he was too busy fixing the long wooden seats.

*****

We saw Pauley running toward our wagon, waving his full pail of red berries. He was yelling as loud as he could for us to stop. Uncle Johan pulled hard on the reins and yelled 'whoa'. The black horsey neighed, looked back at Uncle Johan, and stopped under a great big oak tree.

Pauley ran to my side of the wagon and pointed at the low orange sun. He said there was a man near those trees that had some funny feathers sticking up out of his head! Pauley yelled that the man was riding a horse that did not have a saddle. He was pointing at the man and laughing so hard, he spilled some of his berries.

Uncle Johan looked toward the West. He saw the man, nodded his head, and told us that the man on the horse was an Indian. He said we will be seeing more people like him as we get closer to the lake. We will be seeing lady Indians, too.

As soon as he said that, a boy about the age of Pauley ran out of the bushes. He was funny, too! This young Indian had only one feather sticking out of his head!

Marri laughed louder than I did! They were kind of far away, but we could see they both had really bad sunburns.

*****

Uncle Johan says we will be stopping soon. I heard him tell Mama that we will have gone five long miles by that time. He told me the horsey needs a good night's rest, too. I will need a gooder night's sleep by that time!

*****

Our wagon was under a great big old tree, not too far from a small creek. The trunk of the tree was so big that Marrie, Pauley and I, holding hands, could not reach around it. It was nice that Uncle Johan let us play a little before he gave us a job.

The three of us were running around, picking up all the small branches and pieces of wood we could find. Uncle Johan said we would get a nice surprise if we got enough wood to make a fire for Mama.

Later, Uncle Johan showed Pauley how to brush our horsey and how to tie a rope around its neck. He let Pauley hold the stake that they pounded into the ground. They tied the horsey to it. Uncle Johan said that it would keep the horsey from running away. I never knew he was so smart.

Pauley went with Uncle Johan to the creek later, too. They filled the water barrel first, then brought Mama some water for the bean soup she was boiling on the fire.

*****

We had all the bean soup we could eat; it was not my favorite thing. I thought it was the only food we would get, so I ate more than I really wanted. But I was glad I did it.

Mama gave us the surprise Uncle Johan said we would get. She jumped down from the wagon and showed us a small box, tied with string. She opened the box and took out a big piece of pink bacon. This was our surprise; Mama was going to make us her special kind of bacon-bread. Hungarian style! Yum!Yum! I was so happy, I gave Marri a hug!

*****

We were laying on the blankets in the back of the wagon. Pauley picked the special place to go to sleep; under the long seat near the front. Mama wanted Marri and me to lay down closer to the front too, because there was no canvas cover at the back of the wagon.

Before I fell asleep, I heard Uncle Johan tell Mama that we still have fifteen miles to go in the wagon before we get to this place called Shawnee Bay.

Later, I had a bad, bad dream. I wondered if I would be as old as Marri...before we got to Shawnee Bay and Uncle Tobias.

I laid on my old pillow, the one stuffed with chicken feathers, the rest of the night with my eyes wide open. I could not get back to sleep. I just waited for the sun to come up.

CHAPTER 31

"We miss you, Benjamin."

<u>JULIANNA:</u>

It has only been a little over two days, but I miss my Benjamin so very much. The children feel the same. I can see it in their eyes… and in their actions. We said a special prayer for him before we started the day. Lizzie said her Papa would have loved to eat some of the bacon-bread we had last night.

Even Pauley is trying to be such a good boy. I know he is doing it because he wants to act like a father for Marri and Lizzie. I do not think he knows why he is acting so much older, but I gave him a extra special hug last night. His face turned red when the girls saw us.

Johan said we would not see Benjamin until the end of this week. We all said another prayer for Papa.

*****

It took a little while longer to get everyone in the wagon this morning. Lizzie looked like she did not sleep at all. I believe she may have been so excited about seeing the two Indians yesterday. I heard her coughing a little, too. I prayed she will feel better today. We have such a long trip ahead of us.

Pauley was drinking the last of the berry juice Marri and I made for breakfast. We all had a small taste of it; we did not have this special kind of treat since we left Dombrad.

Johan was making sure our fire that we used to cook the food last night and this morning was put out. He and Pauley went to the creek for some water, and Johan showed him how to put wet sand on the coals, too.

Johan hitched up the horse while the rest of us put our blankets, pots and a few other belongings into the back of the wagon. Pauley said we had enough water in our barrel.

Johan made Pauley feel even better by telling him what a good helper he has become. Then he made the girls happy by telling them how beautiful they looked this sunny morning. Johan knows how to get the most out of my children...even more than I can! Bless him, too.

*****

Oh, yes—I want to tell you one more thing:

Last night, Johan stopped our wagon near a row of tall barberry hedges. They protected the wagon from the slight wind blowing from the North. It also kept our fire from going out too soon last night.

Johan stayed up quite late, keeping the fire going until well past midnight. I looked out at him from the opening of the canvas covering that is behind the seats. I could not believe my eyes! I saw him with a pistol in his hand! He was rubbing the barrel of it on his pants. I saw him put the gun into his belt. He buttoned his black coat to cover it up.

I felt a chill run up my spine. This is our Uncle Johan?

*****

Today is the beginning of our second day. Uncle Johan tells me we have gone about five miles since we started our trip to Shawnee Bay. We still have fifteen more miles to go.

One question still seems to be haunting me:

Why does Johan need a gun?

CHAPTER 32

"Remembering Gran'Papa."

BENJAMIN:

I remember the soldiers, at four o'clock in the morning, breaking in the door of our house. They shot Gran'Papa, took our animals, milk, wine and bread. The soldiers also took most of our belongings. The only thing they let us keep was the clothes on our backs. It was one of the saddest days in my life.

Julianna and I vowed that very night, that if we could survive all of the pain and grief, our family would make it through any hardships we will have for the rest of our lives.

*****

I found out this morning that it was simple to say those words; living up to them was going to be very hard. Our family is going to be separated for at least seven days...perhaps longer. I also found out that being without my family, and Julianna, even for that short period of time, will be more difficult than I could have ever imagined.

*****

Alex, the owner, told me earlier in the week that I could stay here and sleep in the back room of the Trading Post for as long as I wanted. He also said I could use one of the horses in the corral and travel back and forth from the old house we stayed at near the river. I tried sleeping in the stock room for the past two days; I think I will pick out a mare this afternoon and get a good sleep tonight in the old house. Whatever I decide to do will be all right with him. Alex has become one of my best friends in this new land.

*****

During my lunch time, he took me out to the barn, near the corral, and I met a nice man named Tomas. He keeps the animals fed, the horses shoed, and does the general repairs to the Trading Post and all the other buildings.

We talked for quite a while, getting to know each other. He said he has been working for Alex for two years. Tomas said some very nice things about him.

I told Tomas that I was not only to make shoes and boots, but to also try to teach Carl, the one with the long mustache, and his younger brother Kurt, how to repair these same things for the miners and cattlemen. The brothers are pleasant enough to work with, but they do not seem to have a strong interest in learning this craft. Carl is always watching me, but he very seldom picks up any tools. Kurt, on the other hand, asks me a lot of questions. He laughed and asked me what I was going to do with all the money Alex will pay me. He spent part of the day just watching how I sew the boots and cut the pieces of leather for the soles.

I let him trim the edges of a boot and showed him how to polish it. The boot looked brand new. Kurt was so proud of it. He and Carl took the boot to the other room to show Alex.

*****

Tomas said I was doing a good job as he put two cups of coffee on the barrel that I use as a table during my lunch time. We were finally alone. The German brothers always eat by themselves somewhere behind the stables.

Tomas offered me another piece of his wife's apple pie. He looked behind him again, just to make sure no one else was in the room. Tomas was almost whispering now. He told me to be very careful in my dealings with Carl and Kurt. He has heard some bad things about them. He did not know if what he heard was true; he only wanted me to be aware of it.

Tomas did not say any more. We could hear the sound of boots on the wooden floor in the hallway.

All three men came into the room. The brothers were smiling. Alex looked very pleased. He said he had a special announcement for all of us; we could all have the rest of the day off...with pay! We all smiled at each other and thanked Alex.

I told him I had some things to prepare for tomorrow's work. It would only take me less than an hour. We all shook hands again. I could see that Alex was a very happy man.

But I did not like the look on Tomas' face. I wondered why he was not glad for us.

*****

Once I was alone, I lifted out the removable bottom of my hand-made shoe-maker's box. I took out all the maps I had drawn and saved since we left Ellis Island. I smiled as I saw the quality of my drawings on the last two days before we landed near the old house; the maps were becoming more and more professional-looking each day...and more accurate.

I had this rare chance today to compare my maps with some that are being sold at the Trading Post. Alex told me that almost every day, men stop for supplies and maps. Most of the miners and lumbermen are looking for treasure of some kind. Once in a great while, a family will come for a map or directions to Shawnee Bay, which, I see by this new colorful map, is just this side of the lake.

Now I can see my exact location; I can see the direction to Shawnee Bay. Finally I can see this Jamie's Landing that everyone is talking about. It is on the other side of the Lake; the United States side! It is in a place called Pennsylvania!

Now I see. I can see that we are a long, long way from Uncle Tobias and his New York City.

107

*****

This ride back to the old house is pleasant enough. The sun had set long ago. Alex's young colt knows the way, back and forth, by now. Pauley will be happy to know that I named her Queenie.

*****

The sun is bright on the horizon. Queenie is in good spirits this morning. Today is the beginning of my third day at the Trading Post. Only two more days, Julianna, and I will see you soon at Shawnee Bay.

CHAPTER 33

"The third day."

MARRI:

It has been three days since we left the old house. Uncle Johan said he is having a wonderful time being our guide. He is getting to be more fun than we thought he would be. He is not so serious anymore...now that Papa is not with us.

Mama told him we will follow his directions until we meet Papa again near the lake. He was happy she said that. Uncle Johan never had a family before; now he has a play one.

*****

Pauley is getting more excited every day. Uncle Johan told him we will be riding a Ferry when we get to Shawnee Bay. He says it will be a half-day's ride across the lake. The Ferry will carry all of us...AND...our horse and wagon! He says the Ferry will take us to a place called Pen-sill-vane-e-ah. It is in America! Lizzie hugged Mama. She could hardly sit still.

We will ride from this place called Shawnee Bay to a small town on the other side of the lake called Jamie's Landing. Uncle Johan showed us on the map last night; it is about twenty miles from our old house. That is why it is taking us so long to get there.

Mama said we will wait for Papa on the Canadian side of the lake at Shawnee Bay. We want to go to America as a family. Uncle Johan said that was a wonderful plan.

Later, He told Mama that he would do anything to help us get there...even if it meant that we had to wait for Papa a day or more, to come from the Trading Post.

I saw it in Mama's eyes right away; she did not like it when he said that. Why will Papa not be at Shawnee Bay?

*****

I can tell by the sun that it is almost the middle of the day. We are getting tired already. Lizzie is sleeping in Mama's lap. Mama is riding on the seat next to Uncle Johan.

Pauley is running at the side of our wagon, looking for fruits and berries. He is laughing and shouting at Uncle Johan; he can hardly wait to get to the lake.

If we look real, real hard, Uncle Johan says we can see Shawnee Bay in the distance.

Thank you, God.

CHAPTER 34

"More Indians!"

<u>PAULEY:</u>

Early this morning, while we were all sleeping, Uncle Johan went to the woods near the stream we have been following. We heard two loud booms from the shotgun. Mama was trying to get me to wake up; I was real tired from all the bumpy riding and walking yesterday.

Uncle Johan came running out from the tall bushes, waving a rabbit in his hand. He shouted one of those cowboy yells that they do here in America when they are happy. Mama was happy, too. Now we can have some rabbit stew for tonight's supper. I was getting tired of the bacon bread.

Uncle Johan told us to eat our breakfast right away; he said it might rain today, so we should get an early start. It took us less than a half-hour to eat and to get the horse hitched.

*****

I think this is the start of our fourth day on our way to Shawnee Bay. Uncle Johan thanked us for being so good. He seems to like us a little better than before. I do not know why.

I can hardly wait! Uncle Johan said that if the weather is good today, I can take the shotgun for a little while and see if I could shoot a rabbit or a squirrel; He said I did such a good job of finding berries and fruit, that now, I can do some hunting! Oh, MY! Marrie and Lizzie will like that, too. Now they can look for the fruits and berry bushes.

*****

Marri yelled for Uncle Johan to stop the wagon; a horse is coming! He pulled on the reins and yelled 'WHOA'.

She pointed at another Indian with a boy about my age. They were both riding a horse that had only a big red and yellow blanket on it. I thought the horse was funny, too. It was white with big black and brown spots all over it. The most funny thing was the giant turkey feathers on the big Indian's head. It was tied together with a band of beads.

Lizzie laughed, too. She also waved at the young Indian boy. He had a fuzzy fur hat on his head that had a long tail hanging down his bare back. Uncle Johan said it was made from a raccoon. I am not sure if he waved back at us, or shook his clenched fist. Either way, it was funny.

*****

As we got closer to the lake, we saw lots of men, riding in big wagons filled with giant logs. Uncle Johan said they are going to Shawnee Bay too.

He said they were lumberjacks; men in this part of Canada who cut down great big trees, and other men who cut them in smaller pieces. They load the logs onto big wooden wagons—way bigger than ours.

The wagons go from Canada to the lake, and on to the barges, all the way to the United States. Uncle Johan said a lumber mill is being built near Jamie's Landing, so the logs could be cut into lumber for houses and stores. That is the way new towns are made. I did not know our Uncle Johan was so smart. He is almost as smart as Papa. Our Papa makes the shoes for all those men!

CHAPTER 35

"I love Mama so much!"

LIZZIE:

I needed to go potty...real bad. I pulled on the back of Mama's sweater. She knew what to do by the look on my face.

Mama pointed at some trees. Uncle Johan stopped the wagon near the one with the big bush in the front. Mama helped me down and gave me two of the big green leaves from the back of the wagon. I ran behind the bush as fast as I could!

I could hear Uncle Johan telling Pauley to look near the red oak tree for some berries. The tree was on the other side of the wagon. I saw Mama smile at Uncle Johan as she nodded her head. Pauley yelled when he saw some big black ones.

When I was done, Marrie washed my hands with a little of the water from the barrel. Pauley was still picking berries. Uncle Johan told him to jump on the back of the wagon. He said for Pauley to hurry; we still have two miles to go before we can stop for our afternoon resting time

*****

For some reason, the land we were traveling on became dryer the closer we got to the lake. The old wagon was not so bumpy as it was when we started almost four days ago. Even the horsey seems to like the hard ground; pulling the wagon was a lot easier for him, too.

Uncle Johan says we will be at Shawnee Bay in the morning...if all goes well. If all goes well; I wondered why he said that. Maybe later the land will start getting wetter and wetter the closer we get to Shawnee Bay.

I can hardly wait to see the lake. Soon we will be in New York City!

*****

Mama said we had just four potatoes left for tonight's supper. We are going to have them with some of her special bacon bread. Uncle Johan told us that we had some beans in a wooden box under the seat of the wagon, but Mama said we better save them…just in case we need them later.

*****

We sat around the fire, like we always did; each of us eating the bacon bread on a stick. The potatoes were in a pan on top of some hot rocks. We were so happy; Mama made us feel like we were on a picnic.

Mama even told us a story:

She said when I was a tiny baby in our little house in Dombrad, Papa hurt his hand during the winter, and we did not have any big logs for the fire. Mama said she put some baked potatoes in my crib to keep me warm. I could see the tears in her eyes before she was done with that story.

I love Mama so much.

CHAPTER 36

"Our new friends!"

JULIANNA:

The bacon bread tasted so good. Maybe we enjoyed it more today because we could see Shawnee Bay on the other side of those big trees; it was less than a mile away.

Johan was stretched out near the fire, smoking his curved pipe. He was looking up at the stars, pointing at some of the bright ones. Lizzie and Marri were giving each star a special name. Pauley was laying on his back watching them, his head on my lap.

The smell of the bacon must have floated along with the wind. An Indian man and his little girl came toward us. He was walking, holding on to the reins of his young daughter's horse. We could see that she had shoes made of animal skins, decorated with tiny shells.

He held up one hand in the familiar 'peace' sign that Johan taught us. We all held up our hand too, to show that we were friends. Pauley said the Indians might be hungry, so I gave them the last piece of our bacon bread. They ate it real fast. The man nodded his head up and down. I think he liked our Hungarian cooking.

The Indian took some meat out of a big bag that was hanging from his blanket. We showed him how to put it on a stick. We ate some of it too, just to be polite. None of us knew what kind of meat it was...not even Johan.

When we all finished eating, our new Indian friend went and opened a sack that was tied around his horse's neck. He took out some colored beads and gave it to his little girl. She gave one to Marri, Lizzie and a shorter one to Pauley. All the children's eyes lit up like small coals.

We talked to them in our native language. Johan spoke in his mixture of English and German. The Indians smiled and spoke in a very special way. Somehow, we all knew what everyone was trying to say. It was wonderful!

*****

We decided to sleep around the fire tonight. The stars were shining and there seemed to be a cool breeze coming from the lake. The children told me they were too excited to sleep. I looked at them, their bodies curled up in the blankets. They were sound asleep.

Tonight is the end of our fourth day since we left the old house. The days seemed to go by faster than I thought they would; perhaps it was because the children were enjoying themselves, even without their Papa.

Johan whispered to me that we will be at Shawnee Bay before mid-day tomorrow. He saw the happiness reflected in my eyes, I think. Johan reached over to me and squeezed my hand and smiled. At that moment, he was as gentle as my Benjamin.

Johan said he was going to put some wood on the fire. He said 'good night' and went to the other side of the wagon for a few minutes.

Before I went to sleep, I prayed that we would all be together again tomorrow, with Benjamin, at this place by the lake they call Shawnee Bay.

We will be in America soon. Thank you, God.

CHAPTER 37

"A new man!"

BENJAMIN:

Since today will be my last day at the Trading Post, Alex surprised me this morning with a large package that he had placed on my work bench. He looked like a schoolboy; Alex was more excited than I was. He wanted me to open it before I started working on the last of the shoes.

It was a soft package, wrapped with light brown paper, tied with some of the fuzzy twine he uses for all the gifts in the Trading Post. I tore it open as quickly as I could.

I did not know what to say. I just looked at the clothes. Alex was asking me how I liked the black suit and tie. Under the suit was a beautiful white shirt with a fancy pleated front.

Alex knew I was speechless. He told me he was happy to be able to give me the suit. Alex also said I have worked so hard for him and he wanted me to look my best when I returned to my family at Shawnee Bay. Then he surprised me once more!

Alex took a small box down from the shelf above me. Out of the box he took a brand new felt hat. Julianna would have fallen in love with the hat at once. It looked perfect for my new life in America. Alex's smile went from ear to ear.

He smiled when I told him I could never part with my old gray hat; he did not seem to mind.

Later that morning, after he had done the alterations, I stood in front of a floor length mirror. Alex told me to put my old felt hat on. I did look like a new man! He said a new man should have a new name. He said from this moment on, my name will be BEN.

*****

As I rode back and forth to the old house the last few days, I wondered what those big black wires were, being stretched along the top of the poles, on top of things that reminded me of a cross on our church in Dombrad. I have been so busy I did not remember to ask about these funny poles.

I finally asked Tomas what the poles are going to be used for. He told me a crew of men, who have traveled all the way from Jamie's Landing, are installing giant logs along the dirt road that leads from the Trading Post to Shawnee Bay. They call these tall logs 'telephone poles'.

He said in less than two days Alex, and the travelers who come to the Trading Post, will be able to talk to people as far away as New York on the telephone…almost as if they were in the same room with you!

*****

It was late in the afternoon. Alex called me into his office. He said he wanted to tell me some things before I left the Trading Post for the last time.

He said he was very pleased with the way the German brothers are working on the miner's shoes, and how they are finally able to do the simple repairs. With the patterns I have given them, in time, they may become good shoe-makers. Alex said Kurt and Carl had gone home early, but he is sure they would have thanked me for all of my patience and teachings.

Then Alex handed me a small envelope that seemed to be bulging with some paper. He told me it contained $250. in American money. I stood there with my mouth open.

He told me how much he valued our new friendship. He said he will never forget me and my beautiful family. We hugged as only older men do, then he wished that all of our children will have a wonderful life in the United States.

He shook my hand again…and called me Ben. I gave Alex one last hug, wiping away my tears.

*****

I rode to the old house for the last time on Queenie. I did not want to forget this place. It was my family's first safe home since we left Hungary. I wanted to spend one last night here, away from the noise of the Trading Post.

I gathered my few possessions together and put them near the door. I hung up my new suit so it would look nice when Julianna saw me. I even cleaned up my old felt hat. I did not want to forget anything in the morning when I ride toward this fancy place called Shawnee Bay.

I lowered the wick of the oil lamp next to the bed and sat down on the hard mattress. It was almost midnight.

I said a prayer for Julianna, the children, and for their safety. Then I also said a special prayer for Johan, too. His name just came to me…I did not know why.

Now I was ready for my last night's sleep in this house.

*****

I was just starting to fall asleep when I heard a loud pounding on the door. Someone was yelling my name! I did not know who it was!

He was shouting my name…trying to shout it through the door in a loud muted whisper! Ben! Ben! Open the door!

Then I recognized the voice.

It was Tomas!

CHAPTER 38

"How are you? Fine?"

MARRI:

Almost every day, in the back of the wagon, I have been trying to learn new words. The small book I 'borrowed' at Ellis Island has all the words I will ever need in my whole life.

I have been trying to teach Pauley some of the words I think he might need to talk to the boys and men in this new country. So far, he has only learned words that he hears Uncle Johan say lots of times. He does not like to say words that girls might use; he wants to learn the easy words that the miners use here in Canada. I am sure he will change by the time he gets to be my age.

I have discovered that America is made up of a lot of different kinds of people. We are already one small part. I think we will all enjoy learning this funny language.

It is a very cloudy day. Uncle Johan said we should not have any rain until we get to Shawnee Bay. He told Mama this morning that we will be coming near the lake in two or three hours. Sometimes his 'hours' are a long, long time.

*****

We stopped for a little while just to eat some of the meat the Indians gave us last night. It was funny-tasting today, but Uncle Johan said to eat it. He said it would not kill us. I did not like it when he said that.

I went to the back of the wagon again to read more of my book. Near the middle of it, was a map of New York. It is a dot on the map, but it looks a thousand times bigger than our little town of Dombrad.

New York is only one place in America. I cannot imagine how big the United States is. This is our new world!

Later, I showed some of the drawings to Lizzie that were in the back of the book.

The clothes in America are made with lots of colors, like red and blue and yellow. The hats for the men in the book are black or brown, but they wear red and white handkerchiefs tied around their necks; it does not say why.

Men wear hats made of animal skins too, and boots that come up to their knees. They look so funny!

At least Lizzie and me will not have to wear funny feathers in our hair.

*****

As we got closer to Shawnee Bay, I remembered what Mama told me when I was a young girl like Lizzie. She said when we are coming to a special place in our life, or if we are going to do something that we have never done before, that is the time to say a prayer.

I put the book down and wrapped my arms around Lizzie, just like a Mama. She looked up at me, her mouth open, eyes wide as saucers. Lizzie hugged me when I finished the prayer. I hugged her back.

I was happy I remembered that!

CHAPTER 39

"I see the Lake!"

PAULEY:

We were coming to the end of our bumpy, grassy ride. Up ahead I could see a bright yellow road. Uncle Johan told me it was made by mixing sand and clay together. It is nice and hard today, when the sun is shining on it, he said.

That is why he wanted us to come before the rainy season started. Uncle Johan says the rains could be as early as next week. If we would have waited for Papa to finish his shoe-making, he said we might have had to stay at the old house for two more months. I did not know he was so smart.

Uncle Johan turned the wagon to our left, away from the sun. He let me steer the horse on the nice road for just a little while. It was fun to hold the reins, but it was hard work for me. Uncle Johan made it look so easy.

I was glad when he finally told me to let him steer again.

*****

The road made a little curvy turn to the right. It was then we saw it through the trees! I yelled for Mama to look where I was pointing. I stood up from my seat next to Uncle Johan.

We could see the lake! It was so big I could not see the other side of it. The lake was beautiful!

Uncle Johan told us that the Unites States is on the other side of the lake. I was so happy when I heard that, I gave Lizzie a big hug. She was sitting in Mama's lap, next to Uncle Johan. She looked up at me with her mouth open…then she smiled and hugged me back! Mama looked so happy.

Marri had been sleeping in the back of the wagon. She pushed the canvas open behind us and wanted to know why we were screaming. We all pointed at the lake. Marri started to scream, too!

*****

A man on a horse came from behind our wagon. He told Uncle Johan to stop near the big trees up ahead. The man said a 'Stagecoach' was coming. Uncle Johan had to get off the road! I stood up on the seat and turned so I could see.

Four big brown horses, two in the front and two more behind them, were pulling a fancy wooden wagon that had a door on each side. The wagon had bright yellow wheels; smaller ones in the front and bigger wheels in the back. It had a small wire fence around its top, with suitcases and boxes tied to it. A big trunk was tied to the back of the Stagecoach with rope, too.

It had rolled-up curtains on each side of the windows of the two doors. Oh--and the windows did not have glass in them!

A man stuck his head out from one of the windows and waved.

One of the men on top of the high seat was steering the four horses. Another man was sitting next to him. He had a shiny rifle in his arms. Uncle Johan said he helps the driver steer the wagon when he gets tired. He did not tell me why they needed the rifle.

We rode for another one-half hour. It was getting cooler and cooler. Marri said Lizzie was asleep in the back of the wagon. Mama told me to put my coat on.

Then we saw the sign—over there! A big sign, with a giant red arrow painted on the front of it!

SHAWNEE BAY at last!

CHAPTER 40

"Is Papa here?"

LIZZIE:

Marrie was sleeping on the blue and green blanket we brought from the old house. We were both lying on the floor, in the back of the wagon. I was so tired. My head was on Marri's stomach. I could not keep my eyes open. She moved a little when Pauley started yelling. That woke me up right away.

I was coughing just a little bit. Marri turned her body real slow. When she stretched, my head hit the blanket next to her with a loud 'boom'. By now I was wide awake.

I heard Pauley shouting something about a big sign, and a giant red arrow! Is it true? Are we near Shawnee Bay at last?

Mama pushed in on the canvas and told us to come outside. Hurry, she said. I shook Marri. She opened one eye and crinkled up her nose. I told her we are at Shawnee Bay! She sat up real fast and we looked out from the back of the wagon.

There it was at last! Shawnee Bay! I could not read the words, but I knew what that big sign was telling us.

We saw four small buildings; they were all made out of big brown logs. Next to the biggest one, there was a long barn with some horses behind some wood fences. Pauley pointed out the lake to us. It was on the other side of the big building. I never saw any water so big in my whole life!

There was the big sign that said SHAWNEE BAY. Uncle Johan told us that. Next to it was the giant red arrow that was pointing at a great big boat; it was the Ferry we will be riding on today or tomorrow. That is what Uncle Johan told us!

He said we will have to drive our wagon and the horsey onto a barge, one of the big floating islands near the small building. The

Ferry will pull that barge, the one that is tied to it, across the lake...
to Pennsylvania! Then we will be in America!

I was so happy! I hugged Mama and Marri!

Will we see Uncle Tobias by tomorrow?

Maybe, said Uncle Johan. He asked Mama who had the money
to pay for the ride on the Ferry and the barge. Pauley looked at me.
Marri looked at me, too.

We all looked at Mama.

Where is Papa?

I started to cough again.

CHAPTER 41

"Surprise! Surprise!"

JULIANNA:

Johan got off the wagon to go and find out what time the next ferry was leaving Shawnee Bay. He told me he would only be a few minutes. He said to make sure the children do not go off by themselves; there are always strange people traveling in this part of the country, looking for passage into the United States. Then Johan said it would be best to keep them in the wagon until he gets back.

We sat in a circle inside the wagon. The canvas top shielded us from the wind that was blowing in from the lake.

I always say a small opening prayer; I thanked God for getting us safely to this strange land. I said a prayer for Johan and how he has helped us find our way through the mountains and woods of Canada. Then I tried to have each of the children say something that was very special to them since we left the old house. They always surprised me with their innocence and wisdom. I can see them growing into wonderful Americans.

Where are you now, Benjamin?

*****

After we finished our prayers, Pauley said this place has a very funny name; Shawnee Bay—what does that mean. I told him I did not know. I asked Marri if the book she brought from Ellis Island said anything about Shawnee Bay.

Marri opened the back of the book, looking for letters that started with an 'S'. It took her only two minutes to tell us that the word Shawnee sounds like the word Shunye. In America, it is pronounced Sonny or Sunny.

Lizzie told her she would be a good teacher some day. Even Pauley smiled and nodded his head.

Marri has been teaching us from the book she took from the restroom on Ellis Island. She learned how to say 'how are you?' in American words. She taught Lizzie and Pauley how to say the words, too. I am still having trouble sounding out some of the words...but I will learn. Marri told me later that when she earns some money, she will send it to Ellis Island to pay for the book. I am so proud of her. Yes...she will be a good teacher.

*****

I told the children to play with their ball but to stay near the wagon. I was waiting for Johan to come back from the small building that had the big red arrow sign on its roof.

Marri threw the ball over Pauley's head. Pauley turned around and saw that Johan had caught it as he hurried toward us. He said he has wonderful news! We can take the Ferry and the barge and be at Jamie's Landing today before dark. The man at the ticket office said it will be raining most of the day tomorrow. All he needs is the money to pay for the fare, and then to drive the wagon and horse on to one of the barges.

I told him we are not going without Benjamin. We can wait one more day. We can sleep in the wagon tonight.

Johan said he knows Benjamin will not be here today. He said he will pay the fare to get us to Jamie's Landing.

We are not leaving without him, I said again. He is the only one of us that has the money to pay our way to America.

Johan said Benjamin might not be here at all.

CHAPTER 42

"Carl & Kurt!"

BENJAMIN:

Tomas knocked again, then he pushed in on the door; he could not wait for me to open it. He was out of breath.

Two men are right behind him, he said. They want all of the money Alex gave me! I must leave now!

He said Kurt and Carl are less than one hour away. They are both bad men! They have been told to beat me if I do not give them the money!

They will take my horse too, if I do not give them the money, Tomas said. Then I may not be able to get to Shawnee Bay, or Jamie's Landing. He said I should get my belongings and leave now before the men get here!

How do I know I can trust you, I asked.

You have no other choice, was his answer. Carl and Kurt work for a very bad man too, he said.

Who, I asked. Do I know him?

Perhaps you do. His name is Johan.

*****

I had the coffee made hours ago so I could get an early start. I poured another cup of my special black brew for Tomas. We were sitting at the table across from the sink. He was not sure I had made the right decision to wait for Carl and Kurt.

I sat near the door. I wanted to be able to hear them when they came up the one step of the porch.

Tomas could not understand how I could be so calm when I

knew these men were after me. He said he brought a gun from the Trading Post...just in case. He showed it to me; the barrel of the gun was pushed into his belt.

I gave him the only answer I had; it was an answer given to me by a higher source:

We ran from the shootings and the killings in our little village of Dombrad, I said. Julianna and I do not want to run from people anymore. We want to make a new start in this new land; that means we will never again run from people who want to harm me or my family.

I was surprised when Tomas started to tell me about how he and his wife wanted to come to the United States, too. Their two children were killed in an explosion one night. A steamer, loaded with refugees, burst into flames soon after his family boarded. I found out that the Germans were in the same kinds of trouble as we were. Tomas told me that his wife wanted to leave Europe as soon as possible and start a new life in America. He said she died on the ship as they were coming to the United States five years ago. They did not let Tomas in at Ellis Island either. He had to get the help of some men in a trawler---just like my family and I had to do.

Tomas told me that my family is not the first that he has helped come into the United States illegally. He said he and his wife had to endure the same kind of hardships in Germany as we did in our homeland. He told me that his sponsor failed to come and support them when he landed in New York at Ellis Island. He had to find his own way into the United States...just the same as we are trying to do.

I poured Tomas another cup of coffee as I waited for the two men. Then I heard the scrapings of shoes on the wooden porch. There was no doubt it was Kurt and Carl.

I asked Tomas to wait for me in the loft while I talked to the men. I told him not to worry. He got up slowly and went across the room toward the rickety stairs.

*****

I went to the door. I did not know what to expect. The two men stood on the porch for a few seconds, not saying a word. Then Karl extended his hand as he smiled at me. We shook hands. I looked up at Curt; he put his giant arms around my shoulders and gave me the biggest hug I have ever had in my life. I could not hold back the tears.

We sat down at the kitchen table. They started to tell me how grateful they both were for me teaching them how to make an honest living. Carl said that by just watching me and my family work so hard—and being so trustful of everyone—somehow touched their lives, too. They thanked me for teaching them a trade. They thanked me for making them new men!

Then they told me that...yes...they were ordered to get the money that Alex paid me for my work at the Trading Post. They were told to get the money. It did not matter what they had to do to get it back, said Kurt.

I sat back in the chair, my arms on the table, not knowing what was going to happen next. Who was the person that told these men to take away my hard-earned money? My mind went blank.

Carl reached across the table and grabbed my hand.

*****

Kurt looked up as Tomas ran down from the loft and yelled at him to put the gun down! He told Tomas not to harm me. He and Carl were here to help...not to hurt me!

Tomas stopped near the table, close to where I was sitting. I could see the tears in his eyes, too. He threw the gun on the table and embraced the brothers.

I was numb. I sat down while Tomas told me that they are all working for a man named Heinz, and have worked for him for the past two years. It seemed like an easy way to make a living; getting all the money they could from the immigrants that could not pass through Ellis Island.

Then Curt told me something I did not expect; he and Karl changed their minds about robbing me. He said they learned to love people again, once they got to know us. He put his hand on mine and vowed that they will do everything in their power to see that no harm will come to me or my family.

Tomas said that the brothers will have to go back to the Trading Post tonight; they have many shoes to repair. He said it would be better that way, just in case one of Heinz's men would be looking for them.

I gave the men another firm handshake, thanked them for changing their lives because of Julianna and the children; I know I did not have much to do with it...or did I, Lord?

Kurt and Carl went out the door. I do not think I will ever see them again.

*****

Tomas said he will go with me to Shawnee Bay in the morning. He told me he will be back here in a few hours. We should leave at sun-up, so we can be at Shawnee Bay early in the morning. Tomas saw that I was all packed and ready.

He picked his gun up off the table. We shook hands one last time as he hurried out the door.

I wanted to get to Jamie's Landing as soon as possible. Johan has a gun. He is with Julianna and the children. I pray that he is protecting my family. Is he with us...or against us?

God only knows.

I can hardly wait for the dawn.

CHAPTER 43

"One step closer!"

MARRI:

I was lying in the back of the wagon last night, staring up into the sky. It looked like Uncle Johan would be right; it was getting cloudy and it might rain by morning.

I began thinking about the bad soldiers that took my pet goose and all the things I loved. I remembered the bad German soldier who had tied Gretta to the back of their wagon. I was thinking that if I had a gun then, I know I could never have shot that man like they did my Gran'Papa.

When I closed my eyes, I started to think about how bad those soldiers were. I told myself that I did not want to ever see another German person as long as I lived.

Then I remembered what Uncle Johan told us last week: He said the German soldiers were only doing what they were ordered to do. They did not want to be in a war any more than the rest of Europe.

He said the German people had to flee their homes, too...just like Mama and Papa. The Germans are good people; just like we are. I think Uncle Johan is German. I did not want to ask him today.

I began thinking about Henry and Karl, the boys we met on the ship. They were nice German boys. Karl was almost fifteen. They were coming to the United States, just like Papa and our family. I am sure that their wish is to one day be an American citizen.

I began to think some more. I could marry an American some day. Perhaps I could marry Karl...if I ever saw him again.

He was very nice---and very handsome!

I think I will tell Uncle Johan that I love him, too.

*****

Shawnee Bay is not as beautiful as I thought it would be. The buildings are old, the Ferry needs to be painted, and there are a lot of old dirty men standing around, looking at us. I will be happy when we can get to the other side of the lake. Uncle Johan says we will like it on the other side so much more. That is where Jamie's Landing is. It is in Pennsylvania. That is a tiny part of the United States! Horray!

Mama said we will wait for Papa to come with us. She is praying that it will be tonight or tomorrow. She told Uncle Johan that we have no money. She said Papa has the money to pay for our fare.

I wonder why she said that.

*****

While I was doing all this thinking, I began to wonder if anyone else knows about the money Mama sewed in the back of Lizzie's doll. She does not want Uncle Johan to know about that money for some reason.

Perhaps I should take it out...and put the money some place else.

Humm. Maybe I should!

CHAPTER 44

"I am getting tired!"

<u>PAULEY:</u>

Shawnee Bay is not a very nice place. The buildings are all older than that old house we left days ago.

We sat in that bumpy wagon for almost four days to get here. We did not sleep very much. I can hardly wait to get out of Canada. At least that is the way I feel right now.

We have lots of time to wait. Mama said she does not want to go on the ferry and the barge without Papa. She told Uncle Johan that we have no money to pay for it. That is why we are waiting for Papa. He will have lots of money when he comes to Shawnee Bay. We will be so happy to see Papa again!

*****

While we were traveling, Uncle Johan showed me how to draw a map. Today, he showed me how to chop a small 'L' into the birch trees as we walked through the woods. He says that way, we would not get lost if we wanted to find our way back home sometime. He said he learned that from the Indians.

Later, he told me he wanted to be a lumberjack and cut trees in Canada. He said it was very hard work. Uncle Johan said he hurt his back, and had to look for another kind of work.

He said then he got a job working for a man named Heinz soon after that. He liked working for him for a few months, but now...he is not happy working for him. I do not know why. He did not want to tell me. All of a sudden, Uncle Johan looked very sad.

*****

I went to play a game with a stick and a barrel hoop. I saw a boy playing with it this morning. It looked like fun. He started to teach me how to play with the metal ring. Marrie and Lizzie came to play with us, too. We were having a good time!

While I was resting, I saw a man ride over to Uncle Johan. He got off his horse and started to talk to him. I knew the man; I saw him once before at the Trading Post.

They talked all the while we were playing with the new boy. I do not think Mama saw the man talking to Uncle Johan.

I did not know that Uncle Johan has so many friends in this new country.

*****

Mama called all of us to come by the wagon. We were tired of playing with the hoops anyway.

Uncle Johan was standing next to Mama. He told us that we are going on the next ferry and barge to Jamie's Landing. He said we are leaving in one hour.

I do not know who is paying for our ride to Jamie's Landing. I could see the tears in Mama's eyes.

Where is Papa?

CHAPTER 45

"Shawnee Baby!"

LIZZIE:

The closer we got to the lake, the more times Pauley called me SHAWNEE BABY! SHAWNEE BABY! Uncle Johan taught him how to say it. I did not like it…at first.

Now that we are here, I like the special name. I even told Mama that I am the first person that was ever called by that name. I was so happy! I jumped off the wagon and gave Pauley a big hug. He did not know what to say then; the only time I ever hug him is when it is his birthday. He smiled at me funny.

*****

Pauley was playing a new game with a boy we met this morning when we got to Shawnee Bay. The boy's Papa gave them two round metal rings he took off of a barrel, and two wooden sticks. Each boy ran after his own metal ring as he was hitting it with a stick. They were rolling the rings just like they were wheels. It looked like a lot of fun.

The boys looked at Marri and me watching them, then Pauley surprised us both; he said we could play, too.

The boy showed us how to do it. At first Marri rolled it at me, then we rolled the ring at each other. Then we started to roll the rings at the boys. Pauley said it was fun watching us trying to roll the big round things. We all started to laugh!

Pauley said he could teach the Indian boy how to roll the hoops later. He knew we had a lot of time left while we are waiting for Papa. Pauley has been so nice to me today.

I think I am going to like this country.

*****

Uncle Johan said we are going on the ferry and the barge across the lake to America...in less than one hour! I did not see Papa. Mama looked like she had tears in her eyes. She wiped her face like she was chasing a bug. They were tears; I know.

I started to cough. Marri looked at me while Uncle Johan told Pauley that he would have to go with him on the barge to stay with the horse and wagon. Then he said Mama is going to stay on the ferry with me and my sister.

I felt like I was going to throw up. Marri saw that my face was getting kind of green. I coughed again. She took me behind the wagon and told Mama I had to go potty.

*****

I saw some little girls in fancy dresses getting on the ferry. They looked so pretty. My dress was mostly black, with a small white stripe around the bottom. It was dirty, too. I did not want to stand near those pretty girls. Mama wondered why.

I do not know where Mama got the money for us to go on the ferry and barge ride. My doll Gizza still has the money that Mama put inside of her. I know, because I can feel it. She sewed it inside my doll's apron before we left Dombrad. Mama said we are never to use the money...only if Papa says so.

I remember yesterday Mama told us and Uncle Johan that Papa was the only one who had any money for the ferry and barge ride.

Do we have a new friend?

CHAPTER 46

"All aboard!"

JULIANNA:

Dear God...

I remember what Johan told us a few days ago. That is what has kept us from being sad. I remember when he told Marrie that once we get across the lake, she will be in the Unites States of America. Our whole family will be protected by the 'Beautiful Lady'—the Statue of Liberty—from anything bad happening to us in this new country. She was so happy to hear that from Johan! God bless him...and Benjamin. Amen.

*****

I did not want to stand with the children at the front of the ferry as it left Canada. All the other children and their parents, with their pretty dresses and coats, were waving to people as the ferry and the barge moved away from the long wooden dock.

Pauley and Johan were on the barge that was tied to the back of our ferry. They had to stay with the horse and wagon. One man told Johan that it will only take about four hours to get to Pennsylvania. My...that is a strange word!

I took the children to the back of the boat. I wanted them to watch our old world...one last time.

The barge was tied to the back of the ferry with a long heavy rope. We could see Pauley and Johan waving at us behind the fence on the back of the barge. That looked like fun.

139

*****

Johan told me last night that the man on the horse talking to him was a Pony Express Rider. I did not know what that meant... until Pauley told me. He said Johan was trying to explain to him what the Pony Express Rider does. He rides all across Canada to deliver mail, packages, and other important things. They have been doing this for a long time. But now, Johan said that soon there will not be any more riders. Those poles we saw with the black wires on them are going to take the place of these men. The Pony Express is being replaced with the telephone. He did not have time to tell us any more, but he said we will be able to talk to Uncle Tobias who is in New York City, on this machine, while we are in Pennsylvania. I cannot believe it; God truly works in miraculous ways!

*****

The ferry started to blow its whistle. It blew four long loud sounds, just like a screaming child. We were at Jamie's Landing... at last! This new world looks so exciting!

Johan told us that this was an Irish town. I did not know exactly what that was, but I have never seen anything like it in my entire life! And I have never heard so much noise before.

After the ferry landed, the people started to get off at the dirty grey-green dock. It took them a long time to get all of us passengers and our things unloaded. As soon as that was done, it pulled ahead so the people on the barge could get their wagons and horses off.. I could see that the children, especially Pauley, enjoyed that part of the trip.

Jamie's Landing was not too much longer than the barge and the ferry put together. There were three or four small shops at the far end of the town. A building that had a big star on its top was in the middle. I found out later that this small building was the town Sheriff's office. Johan explained what his job was in this exciting place.

The last two long buildings were for the dance halls, the saloons, and the dress shops for the women who 'worked' in the dancing places. I have never seen such a town in all my days!

On the roof of the building nearest the dock was a big sign: THE FIRST 2 DRINKS ARE FREE—ROOMS TO LET!

We could hear piano music coming from the building; some of the music also came from the open upstairs windows. Two or three women in fancy dresses were leaning out of those windows, singing and yelling at each other. Another group of men and women were sitting on a large balcony overlooking the stables, where they keep horses and mules. On the other end of the building was a wagon repair shop.

Two of the women who were leaning out of the upstairs windows were waving and shouting at us. One of them called Johan's name. She looked like she had hardly any clothes on. He waved back. Johan said he was only trying to be polite.

I asked Johan what those girls did in that building, with all their singing and screaming and waving to everyone. He said it was better that I did not know.

The children, with their mouths open and eyes wide as saucers, did not say a word. I could not imagine what they were thinking at this very moment.

A beautiful blonde-haired woman, about my age, walked toward us. She shook my hand and told me her name was Lily. Then she hugged the children and said how beautiful they were. Pauley's face got all red. Lily shook Johan's hand. I could see in their eyes that they were old friends.

Lily told us that she has a room downstairs for special guests like us…and friends of people like Johan. The room was behind the kitchen. Lily said the children might like to sleep on the larger bed and I could have the smaller cot in the corner.

Johan asked if he could sleep in the barn. The hay is nice and warm this time of year; at least that is what he told us.

Pauley wanted to know if he could sleep with his Uncle Johan. I told him it was a good thing to do; he could keep Johan from being lonely.

*****

Lily took us to the back of the building, then into a long hallway. She unlocked the door at the end of the hall and we followed her into a large room.

The first thing we saw was this strange small machine on the table near the bed. It was a black thing with lots of long wires coming from the back of it. The wires went into the wall. Lily said the machine was connected to those long poles at the sides of the road. She said it is the new telephone everyone is talking about; we could talk to anyone in the United States if they had a telephone, too. Oh, my!

Lily said we must all be very tired. She told the children to go into a corner bedroom. They could wash up in the tiny room that had a sink for washing your hands, and a fancy seat for going potty. Marri and Lizzie hurried in to see all those wonderful new things!

I wanted to see them for myself, but before I could, Lily asked me a very frightening question:

Did I know that a man with a gold tooth was looking for me and my family? A man named Heinz is waiting for you and your husband…in the kitchen.

I sat down and stared straight ahead. I could not speak for a moment. I could only think about the safety of Benjamin and our children.

The door to the kitchen opened.

Heinz was coming toward me.

I closed my eyes.

CHAPTER 47

"The hand of God."

<u>BENJAMIN:</u>

Before I went to bed, I cleaned my old gray felt hat. I wanted it to look nice when I got on the ferry with all those fancy people Tomas kept telling me about.

I had a choice: wear my new suit—or put it into one of my black bags. I decided I better wear the suit.

*****

I did not sleep as well as I thought I would. All night long, I kept thinking about Julianna and the children. I was not worried about them; I knew they were being protected by a power much greater than I could ever provide. I think I could not sleep because I missed them so very much.

*****

Last night, I had put all of my things in two black bags. I tied them up this morning, and put the bags on the floor near the side window. While I was waiting for Tomas, I was checking every corner of the house; I did not want to leave any of the children's favorite home-made toys behind.

Once in a while, I looked through the cracked pane of glass to see if Tomas was coming around the big oak tree.

Tomas was true to his word; I could hear him ride up to the old house. As soon as I heard him on the porch steps, I opened the door. We shook hands and he helped me take the bags outside, tying one behind the saddle of each horse.

We had a four-hour ride ahead of us to Shawnee Bay if we only stopped for a short while to rest the horses.

I said a silent prayer as we rode away. I looked back at the old house one last time. These moments will stay with me for as long as I live. I believe they will be part of our most precious memories someday.

*****

We stopped near a small brook and let the horses drink from the cool water, but only for a little while; both of us were anxious to get to Shawnee Bay.

Tomas sat down on a large rock next to the water's edge. He offered me a part of his home-made sandwich. I did not have anything to eat up to this time, so I took a big bite. It would be enough to get us all the way to the lake.

I told him that I will repay him when we get to Shawnee Bay. He said no; he was happy to be able to help me and my family. That look in his eyes was very special.

While we were eating, Tomas pointed at those big bare trees on one side of the road in the distance. I said they had what looked like black ropes hanging from them…as far as the eye could see. He told me they were not ropes, but electrical wires for a new miracle machine called the TELEPHONE.

A miracle such as this was unheard of in Hungary. I asked Tomas what this machine did for the people in this country and the United States.

He said it is possible to use the telephone to talk to people all over the United States, if the person they want to talk to also has a telephone. Tomas saw the tell-tale expression in my eyes. He then told me that I might be able to talk to our Uncle Tobias in New York City—if he has a telephone! We may be able to find out that information when we get to Jamie's Landing across the lake. So far, Shawnee Bay, in Canada, only has mail delivered by Pony Express riders. It would take about one month to get a letter to New York.

I was excited about this new revelation. I told Tomas that we should get back on our horses. I wanted to ride to Shawnee Bay as soon as possible. I wanted to see if it was possible to talk to our Uncle Tobias on this special thing they call the telephone.

Tomas said it is a marvelous piece of equipment. Most of the time, it works. Sometimes, the Indians cut the wires and the telephone cannot be used. They do it for fun. The Trading Post gives the Indians fruits and vegetables if they do not climb on the wooden poles to damage the lines. Tomas said we are beginning to get along with them a lot better that way.

*****

We finally got to Shawnee Bay one hour after the ferry departed. The people in the Ticket Office told us they have only two crossings today to Jamie's Landing.

Tomas checked with a man wearing a round red cap and was told that we could wait for the ferry to come back in the diner. It was at the back of the small wooden building with the big sign on its top. He told us too, that the ferry is leaving again at three o'clock this afternoon. He said "Do not be late, 'cause they do not wait". He gave us a big, friendly smile.

We could be at Jamie's Landing before dark.

*****

We took the man's advice and walked in the road to the other end of the log buildings, holding on to the reins of our horses. We passed a small cabin that had a star painted on its front door. The place to eat was at the far end of the buildings, not too far from the loading dock.

We tied the horses to the posts near a water trough; the horses needed a cool drink, too.

One of the men in the coffee shop told Tomas that we could take our horses to the stable and they would be fed and watered

145

until it was time to take the ferry. The man told us it was just on the other side of the saloon.

*****

We finished a fine meal of steak and potatoes. Tomas paid for our meals. Do not argue he said. I thanked him. The look in his eyes told me Tomas would be a life-long friend.

Before we got up to leave, a tall man came toward our table. I recalled seeing him before, but I could not remember where. Was it on the trawler?

He looked at me, then asked if my name was Benjamin.

Tomas told me what he said. I nodded.

Then he said a man will be waiting for me at Jamie's Landing. He is looking for me and my family. His name is Heinz. He will be waiting for you at a place called Lily's.

The man hurriedly left the diner.

Tomas repeated his words to me so that I understood every thing that was said. I sat down again. Tomas stood next to me. He put his hand on my shoulder.

I found myself starting to pray in the middle of this old building. I knew that Julianna and the children are waiting for me at Jamie's Landing. I looked up at Tomas and said we have nothing to fear. I truly believed it.

Tomas whispered a soft 'Amen'.

CHAPTER 48

"My Prayers."

MARRI:

Lizzie did not want to come out of the little fancy room in Aunt Lily's house for a long time; she was having so much fun. She kept turning all the knobs and handles. They all made their own funny noises, and every one of them did something special. Even Pauley wanted to come into the room. Mama told him he could go in later. Lily said people call it the 'bathroom'.

I know why Pauley wanted to come in; he wanted to see Lizzie or me in the beautiful white tub. It had big red and pink flowers painted all over its bottom. Mama fell in love with it right away. Aunt Lily was so happy when Lizzie hugged her.

*****

I wonder what Papa is doing right now. I truly miss him.

When I was a little girl, Papa taught me to look up at the sun or the moon when I needed to pray for the Lord's help. He was right; God seems so much closer to me then.

When I see Papa praying, I see him taking off his hat and wiping the inside of the hat band. I do not think he even knows he is doing it...but he does it every time. I think it makes him feel closer to God.

I pray that Mama and Papa will not have any more bad things happening to them in this new country. In Dombrad, I saw it in their eyes; they were growing older and older every day. I am so happy we will soon be together again in America. Then I will see Mama and Papa start growing younger and younger again.

Thank you, God.

*****

I heard Papa tell Mama, a long time ago before we left our old house, that the money in Lizzie's doll is all American money. It was sent to Papa by Uncle Tobias for us to use when we try to come into the United States. Papa said it is so much better to have American money than Hungarian. Papa said lots of people in this new country will not take paper money if it is not American dollars. Uncle Tobias told Papa the truth.

I thought about that for a long, long time.

*****

OH—I was going to take the money out of Lizzie's doll and hide it where no bad people could find it.

I prayed and prayed to do the right thing.

I did not take the money out of Lizzie's doll.

I think God gave me the right answer!

CHAPTER 49

"YEEE-HAAA!"

PAULEY:

I was standing by the dock, watching for Papa; Uncle Johan told me to do it. He has to go back to Lily's to take care of Mama and my sisters. He said Papa will be at Jamie's Landing before dark. All kinds of people pass by these old buildings on their way to the United States. Uncle Johan told me he would be back to get me in about one hour. I know I will be hungry by that time. He is always on time.

I saw some more Indians walking by. I thought it would be fun to talk to them, but they have their own language. No one knows what they are saying, so it is not so bad; they do not understand it when we speak to them in Hungarian, either. But they like it when I say 'UGH"! They know how to say that word, too. Uncle Johan said he things it means 'Hello'.

*****

I did not see Papa, but I could see this shiny black thing coming down the middle of the road. A man saw me looking at it with my mouth and eyes wide open. He told me it was a car. It did not have a top.

Two people were riding in it; a man with a big black mustache, and a fat lady with a great big hat. She had one hand on top of her head, trying to keep her hat from flying off.

The man was steering with a big wheel, sitting on the front left side of the machine...I mean the car. They were sitting on one long black padded seat. The car was making a lot of funny-sounding noises as they drove down the middle of the dirt road. Every once in a while there was a popping noise, too.

Someone said the car was from the United States. I could not read the name on it, but it started with a 'W'.

The man standing next to me said the owner of the car comes to get fuel for it every week from a trawler that stops at Jamie's Landing. He told me that pretty soon, people will not need the Pony Express riders anymore.

I thought it was funny when the driver of the car drove past us and yelled, 'YEEE-HAAA'!

*****

I kept watching and watching, but still no sign of Papa.

I saw another man go by today with a mule. He tied a pick, a shovel, and lots of brown sacks on his mule's back. He said he was going to go into the mountains and search for gold. He did not tell me why. What is gold?

*****

I waited for Papa some more. It was way past the time Uncle Johan said he would be back. I got worried...then I got scared. Maybe he was hurt, or Mama got sick.

I did what a man should do; I ran all the way to Lily's place as fast as I could. I ran to the back of the building where Mama and my sisters were waiting.

I saw Uncle Johan running down the hall. He had a gun in his hand, running toward Lily's room. He looked back at me for a second, then yelled that someone told him the man with the gold tooth was in the room with Lily...and Mama!

CHAPTER 50

"I SEE THE GUN!"

LIZZIE:

Mama told me and Marri to wait in this tiny bathroom until she calls us to come out. She needed to talk to Aunt Lily she said. I do not know why we are calling her 'Aunt'. I did not know we had one in the United States already.

I threw up again. I was coughing more, too. I try to hide it from Mama, but Marri said she was going to tell if it does not get better soon.

Uncle Johan said he has an old German recipe that can cure my cough. He told me not to worry…so I am not going to.

*****

Marri said I could go outside and play with Louie, our new friend. Mama and Lily were still talking in the big bedroom where we are staying. We could hear them, but Marri said she could not understand what they were talking about.

I went out of the small door at the side of the bathroom and saw Louie standing on the corner, waiting for one of us to come out and play. He is from France. I do not know if that place is in Canada, or if it is in the United States. He talks funny, but we like to play the barrel hoops game with him.

While I was chasing a barrel hoop, I thought about the day last week when Uncle Johan asked me a strange question. He wanted to know if I knew who, in our family, had the money hidden away. I told him Pauley has it. By the look on his face, I think he was surprised to hear that.

I did not tell him I was only joking. I do not know if Uncle Johan knows that Mama put the American money inside my doll. He told me he knows about the money Papa had sewn inside of his hat, too. I did not know about that.

I was getting tired. I was hoping that Marri would yell and tell me to come back inside. Just then, Louie fell down and skinned his knee. He said he had to go home.

I stood outside near the back of the house and started to think again. There must be some bad people in the United States, too. Uncle Johan has to have a gun. He keeps it in his belt so nobody can see it...but I did. Mama said it is only a toy; but Uncle Johan told me he is going to give it to Pauley so he will have it when we get to New York City.

Papa says too much thinking is no good for anyone.

*****

Marri ran into the street to get me. She said we have to hurry back to Aunt Lily's place...RIGHT NOW!

We ran through the door again that led to the hallway as fast as we could. We saw Uncle Johan with the shiny black gun in his hand. He was running from the front of the building, down the hall---running toward Aunt Lily's room!

I started to scream! My throat got real sore again. I could hardly breathe, but Marri was pulling me down the other end of the hall to Aunt Lily's door.

Then we saw Pauley running down the hall...right behind Uncle Johan---running after him!

Was Uncle Johan going to hurt Aunt Lily?

Where was Mama?

I started to get real dizzy. I though I was going to fall... down... and...die.

CHAPTER 51

"How Great Thou Art!"

JULIANNA:

I had my eyes closed:

I remembered telling Lily about the nightmare our Lizzie had the day her Gran'Papa was killed in Dombrad.

I remembered telling her about our family not being able to come through Ellis Island. Uncle Tobias said it would be so easy. Instead, it has been one month wondering if we would ever see him again.

As I prayed, I remembered reaching out for someone. I felt the warm touch of Lily's hand. I did not know if I was dreaming or not. I still had my eyes closed; I was afraid to open them...for fear of what I would see.

I went out one morning. I took it upon myself to buy the children some candy; they had not had anything sweet for weeks. Lily did not say anything to me when she saw them eating it. Now, when I was thinking about it, she did not ask me where I got the money.

*****

Standing next to Lily, my eyes still closed, I remember her telling me that a friend from Shawnee Bay called early this morning on the telephone; Benjamin was on his way. He will be here late this afternoon. The friend said we will be able to notice him right away; Benjamin will be the only man in Jamie's Landing wearing a brand new suit! But I will know him more by his old gray felt hat. He said one more thing; his new name in the United States of America is now 'BEN.

I felt Lily's hand on my shoulder. I opened my eyes.

*****

Now I was standing, face to face, with the man they call Heinz... the man with the gold tooth. Kurt and Carl were standing on each side of him. Alex, the man who owns the Trading Post, was in the background near the bedroom door.

Lily stood next to me, her arm around my waist. I could feel my body shaking. She held me tighter.

We could hear loud noises coming from the hallway.

I heard Johan's voice...calling out my name!

He pushed in on the door and hurried into the room. Johan was face to face with Heinz, pointing the gun at the man with the gold tooth—or was he pointing it at me?

CHAPTER 52

"LILY'S!"

BEN:

We heard the shrill sounds of the ferry's whistle, letting us know it was time to board the barge. I was so concerned about Julianna and the children that I did not even think who was going to pay for our way on the ferry. Tomas said he will pay for our rides. He wanted to give me a gift for all the trials our family has gone through. I tried to at least give him my share, but he would not accept it. I knew, right then and there, that our bond would last a lifetime.

We were told that we would have to ride on the barge with our horses; or one of us could stay with them, while the other man could then ride the ferry. We decided to ride with the horses. Tomas said we could talk that way, and get to know each other more. I agreed.

*****

Tomas and I stood along the back rail of the barge, watching the giant wheels of the ferry as the water spilled from it. We soon tired of that and sat down on some wooden crates.

Tomas lit his pipe. He said he liked to smoke and talk at the same time. I will get this habit now that I am in the United States he said. The smoke curled above his head, blowing toward the back of the barge.

We talked about the tall man at Jamie's Landing, telling us that the man named Heinz will be waiting for me at a place called 'Lily's'. Tomas said he has heard about the woman called Lily. She can show me how to use the telephone. He heard that this Lily has one in her own room!

We talked briefly about Carl and Kurt. Tomas said they both worked for Heinz for a while...but only to pay for their debt for riding on his trawler from Ellis Island. They said Heinz is a very bad man. Perhaps that is why Johan has the gun; in case Heinz was going to harm my family!

*****

We did not see Julianna or the children on the dock at Jamie's Landing. I closed my eyes for a moment and said a few words in prayer for my family. Tomas did not see me do it. Then again, he may have; as we led the horses off the barge, I believe I saw him saying his own silent prayer.

We hurried to the Pony Express office. Tomas asked the man at the counter if he knew where we could find a woman by the name of Lily. He said yes...everybody in town knows about Lily's place. She is a popular lady. He looked at us with a funny smile. She is a friend of a man named Johan...and very good friend of a big burly man by the name of Heinz. He said he heard that they have known each other for quite some time, and have worked together for almost five years

This must be the Heinz that I have come to know; the man with the gold tooth...the man that took our money.

I told the man that I think I know this person...Heinz.

He said we got to Jamie's Landing just in time. He is at Lily's right now...along with two other rough-looking men.

Tomas and I ran out of the Pony Express office! We heard the music coming from the building at the end of the road. There it is! 'LILY'S'!

Where are Julianna and the children?

CHAPTER 53

"HE IS HERE!"

MARY:

The most fun we have had, I think, was when we tried to talk to the Indians. Lizzie and I said a lot of Hungarian words to the girl Indians, but none of them ever talked back at us. I think they will get spanked by their Mama's if they try to talk to me or Lizzie. They must be sad a lot of times if they do not get a chance to talk to other girls.

Pauley learned some new words. He can speak with the Indians really good. But most of the time, I think he is fooling me and Lizzie; he does not know what they are saying, and they do not understand Pauley either. But they smile and raise their arms and wave at him. He shakes his head up and down and says their favorite word, UGH!

*****

Yesterday, we went to the Pony Express office just to see some people use the telephone. We had to wait and wait for a long time until a man and woman came in to talk on it. Even Mama though it was exciting.

We stood next to the long wooden counter. The man who worked at the office showed them how to use the machine. They were trying to talk to their cousin who lives in Garland. It is someplace in Pennsylvania.

Mama said it would take her a million years to learn how to use a machine like that shiny black telephone.

Lizzie and I just laughed when she said that. I am going to have a telephone in two rooms of my house when I grow up! Lizzie said she will have one in EVERY room!

Pauley told us he will have one in his brand new car when he is old enough to drive. We all laughed some more; no one is going to have a telephone in their car...ever!

*****

I ran into the street to get Lizzie. Mama said to get her and hurry back to Aunt Lily's—RIGHT AWAY!

I saw Lizzie sitting on the edge of the wooden sidewalk. I ran and grabbed her by the hand. I yelled that we have to go back to Aunt Lily's as fast as we can. I could see that Lizzie looked very tired, but I pulled her up anyway and ran toward Lily's Place. Lizzie started to cry.

We ran through the back door. I saw Uncle Johan with the gun in his hand, running at us from the other end of the hall. He was running to Lily's room, too!

Right behind him, Pauley was running toward us. He was trying to catch up to Uncle Johan; I do not know why Pauley was running after him! Was Uncle Johan going to hurt Aunt Lily? Was he going to hurt Mama?

Uncle Johan turned and yelled at all of us: 'The man with the gold tooth is in Lily's room! DO NOT COME IN!'

We looked at him with our mouths open. Then he hurried into the room and slammed the door.

PAPA! WHERE ARE YOU?

CHAPTER 54

"PAPA! PAPA!"

PAUL:

I do not think it was a prayer when he said it, but it seemed to help the man. One of the workers on the barge pinched his hand between two big crates. He yelled out some loud words that sounded like SON-NUM-AH-BEECH-KA!

The man looked like he felt a lot better after he shouted those words. I asked Uncle Johan what they meant, but he would not tell me. I will try to remember those American words. I can ask Uncle Tobias what they mean when I see him.

*****

One thing I have learned since we left our stone house in Dombrad is that I have the best sisters in the whole world; that includes the United States...AND Canada!

I do not know why, but Lizzie and Marri are getting nicer and nicer the older they get. Maybe I am getting to be nicer to them, too. I find myself getting to like my sisters more and more...but I still like to pull Marri's pigtails!

*****

Uncle Johan told me last night that he wants to be my big brother. I think I will let him be one. Yes...at first, I wanted to grow up to be just like our Uncle Johan. He has helped Mama and my sisters and me find our way from the old house, to Shawnee

159

Bay, and all the way to Aunt Lily's place. We are finally at Jamie's Landing, in the United States. We could not have done it without him. Uncle Johan is a very nice man.

But now I see what a wonderful father we have, too. I want to grow up to be just like my Papa!

*****

I was running down the hall as fast as I could after Uncle Johan. Marri and Lizzie were running toward me from the back part of the building.

Uncle Johan yelled at all of us to stop! He said not go in the door to Aunt Lily's room! We have to wait in the hallway until he comes to get us. Do not be afraid!

Uncle Johan opened the door slowly and went in. We did not hear a sound coming from the room.

Marri looked ten years older to me. She was holding Lizzie's hand, trying to be a Mama.

I could hear Lizzie coughing, but she was not crying anymore; I think she was praying that everything is going to be all right. I was not so sure.

*****

We sat in the hallway for a long, long time. Lizzie was quiet by now. She was asleep, her head on Marri's shoulder.

We could hear voices coming from Aunt Lily's room. Sometimes they were loud. Once we even heard some laughing. I wanted to go in, but Marri said 'NO'. We have to wait for Uncle Johan to call us. I suppose she was right.

But where is Papa?

CHAPTER 55

"MY AMERICAN DOLL!"

LIZ:

Before, I used to wait for Mama or even Marri to say our prayers; right now, I was saying my own prayers...for Papa and Mama and our whole family. I closed my eyes.

I think my doll Gizza believes in God now, too.

*****

Yesterday, when Mama and Marri went to the store, Aunt Lily gave me a hug and put me on her lap. She told me I was a pretty little girl. She looked into my eyes and told me that I will be so happy in America. My brother and sister will love to play and go to school in New York City she said. She gave me another big hug!

I looked up at Aunt Lily and told her that she looks like a nice lady, too...the kind of ladies that are in the United States. I told her she reminded me of the 'Beautiful Lady'—the Statue of Liberty—that we saw when we were at Ellis Island.

Aunt Lily started to cry. She gave me a big, bigger hug!

I wanted to make her happier, so I told her my secret:

All the American dollars that Uncle Tobias sent to Papa, for all of us to come to the United States, is sewed into the back of my doll Gizza! There! I finally told somebody! I am so glad!

Aunt Lily was surprised that I told her about the money. She said she was surprised that I even knew there was money sewn into the doll. She gave me a real bigger hug this time.

Then Aunt Lily told me her secret: She knew that the money was in my doll, because Uncle Johan told her. She said the man with the gold tooth first told her about Papa's family two weeks ago. She said they were going to share our money…like they always did. It was fun, she said. Then Aunt Lily told me that she was going to take the money out of my doll tonight…while we were sleeping.

I looked up at her with tears coming down my face. I did not know what to do or say. I gave Aunt Lily another hug.

She said Uncle Johan was going to take the money from my doll last week…but for some reason…he changed his mind. She has not seen him for almost one week.

Then I heard Marri and Mama knocking on the door.

*****

We were sitting in the hall, cross-legged, against the wall. Marri had an arm around me, whispering that everything is going to be all right. Pauley was sitting across from us. He was out of breath, and had tears in his eyes. We could hear loud noises coming from Aunt Lily's room. We heard Mama and Aunt Lily's voices…shouting and screaming! We could hear Uncle Johan, too!

Then we heard the loud voice of the man with the gold tooth! Was that Carl's and Kurt's voices, too? OH, MY!

As we were sitting there, the door at the end of the hall opened. We saw Papa running toward us!

Tomas from the Trading Post was right behind him!

I felt like I wanted to scream!

CHAPTER 56

"DARLING!"

JULIE:

Johan came into the room, the gun in his hand. He was pointing it at everyone, as if he was not sure what Heinz or the other men were going to do. Johan, I know now, was trying to protect me.

Lily was at my side, holding my hand. She looked more surprised than I was. I squeezed her hand until I felt my nails in her flesh.

The first thing Heinz did was grab me around the waist with both arms! I tried to push him away! Then he pulled me toward him...and gave me a great big hug!

All the men started laughing...except Johan. He did not know what to say. Johan looked at Heinz, who nodded his head up and down and smiled at him. I was surprised to see a tiny tear in the corner of Heinz's eye.

Johan finally lowered his gun. He said he ran into the room because he was afraid for my safety. He was so happy to see Heinz with a big smile on his face; I do not think anyone had ever seen him smile before!

Johan put his gun in the pocket of his black coat. He came toward me...and gave me the biggest hug I have had since my wedding day. I was so happy...I hugged him back.

Alex, from the Trading Post, came out of the kitchen. He shook Johan's hand and wrapped his big arms around him, and said this was going to be a day that none of us will ever forget.

He came across the room and took hold of my shaking hands. Then he hugged me, too. Alex smiled as he wiped his tears with a new red handkerchief.

Carl and Kurt were led across the room by Lily. They smiled and bowed from the waist as they kissed my hand. I felt so special.

I could feel my face getting red. What did I do to deserve this kind of attention?

Lily even taught me what is going to be one of my favorite American words...Darling!

Everyone was smiling, talking and shaking each other's hands for what seemed like the longest time. For a moment, I thought I was in heaven. I was so happy. Then, I realized that my children and my husband were not with me. All of a sudden, I was sad beyond belief. I longed for my family.

I think Heinz saw it in my eyes. He came over to me and asked why Benjamin and the children were not with me. Heinz said he wanted to tell Benjamin and our family about the miracle that changed him...and the people working for him.

Johan looked at me with the most startled expression I have ever seen. He said he forgot! The children are waiting in the hallway! They are safe at last! Now they could come in and join the party!

But...where is my Benjamin? Why are we here?

Lily said to be patient; I will know in a few moments.

CHAPTER 57

"I LOVE YOU!"

BEN:

Marri stood up and blocked the door with her arms stretched out. She yelled for me to stop! The children were yelling, 'Do not go in the room, Papa! Uncle Johan said NOT to open the door! STOP, PAPA!'

I turned the knob and pushed the door in!

It slammed against the wall. The children ran in behind me. Lizzie and Marri were screaming, 'MAMA! MAMA'!

Tomas knew what was going to happen all along. He walked into the room behind me, smiling. He went over to Julianna and kissed her on the cheek. Tomas grabbed her by the arm and brought her to me.

He circled his big arms around the both of us. We kissed... and hugged...and cried as the people in the room clapped and shouted our names. The children joined us. We had never seen such happiness in our entire life. What did we ever do to deserve this wonderful surprise?

Johan was the first person to walk over to us. He said he wanted to officially welcome my family to the United States of America. Because he had spent the most time with us, he said all the others agreed that he should be the first to speak.

Lily had five chairs in the center of the room, curved in the shape of a half-moon. Kurt and Carl directed us to our seats and made sure we were comfortable.

The children were so excited; I tried to show them how calm I could be, but could not help myself. I felt my hands shaking as I sat down next to my sweetheart.

Johan came forward. He cleared his throat, smiled at us, and began to speak:

*****

"I am so happy to see all of my friends here, gathered together at Lily's Place. The first thing I want to say to this family is ---I want to beg all of you to forgive me."

He stopped talking for a few seconds. Johan swallowed hard and wiped his nose. We could see the tears in his eyes.

"I was the one who thought of the plan to split up your family. It is always easier to break people's spirits when they do not have their loved ones around them. It has been working for us...and our men...for almost three years."

Marri and Lizzie looked up at me, not understanding all that was happening. Even I did not know what to say. I think I was in shock, too.

"At first, I helped this family to Shawnee Bay and then to Jamie's Landing. During our travels, I took the money out of little Lizzie's doll. We knew that the family could never find their way back to Canada or to the children's Uncle Tobias in New York."

Lily gave Johan a drink of water. He sat down opposite little Lizzie, Pauley and Marri. Johan was sobbing as he spoke.

"Yes, I stole the money out of the doll...but never again! Your family changed me. I put the money back into the doll, without anyone even knowing I took it."

Lizzie got up from her chair and walked over to Johan. She put her hand on his knee...and smiled. Tears flowed freely from their eyes...and ours.

"One day, after I listened to Julianna's prayers, I began to have second thoughts. Then, the day we left the old house, I heard Benjamin praying behind the barn. I knew then what I had to do. It was a wonderful feeling during our trip to Shawnee Bay, when I put the money back. It was also the first time I ever paid for anyone's fare across the lake! I got in touch with Heinz and told him what I had done."

I reached for Julianna's hand.

166

We held each other while Johan continued. He sat upright and cleared his throat again.

"I have one last thing to say. I started out as 'Johan'. That was fine with me. But then, Julie told the children they could call me their Uncle Johan. I put up with that nonsense for a few days…but a strange thing happened; I got so used to it. I was a new man---a more caring man.

I was never an Uncle to anyone before. Now, I am so happy to be…Uncle Johan."

We all got up from our chairs and formed a small circle around Johan, hugging and crying and sobbing tears of joy.

*****

Tomas was the next to speak. He came from the back of the room. He was smiling from ear to ear. Tomas knew what was going to happen at Lily's several days ago:

*****

"I had gone through the same experiences that Benjamin and Julianna have had to endure in the old country. I lost my wife when she got sick on the ship just before we arrived at Ellis Island…but I wanted to go on…for her sake.

"I vowed then that I would help as many families as I could to find a new way of life here in America.

"These people have a love for this country, and they soon became like a family to me. I want to share that love with them and all the other immigrants that come to Canada and the United States of America. God bless Julianna, Benjamin and those beautiful children. Amen!"

Tomas hugged us all. He will be a lifelong friend!

*****

Carl and Kurt came forward and joined us. Tomas gave the girls another big hug, patted Pauley on the back, and hurried to sit down next to Lily on the sofa. She gave him a kiss on the cheek. I could see he was just as happy as we were.

Kurt was the first brother to speak:

*****

"We have been helping Heinz, any way we could, since we came into Canada. We had to do very little for the money he gave us. He said he got paid handsomely by the immigrants.

"Then we found out that he was beating people who did not have enough money to pay him for bringing them into the country through Canada...which was also an illegal thing to do. But Heinz knew they had no choice; it was impossible for these people to turn back."

Carl, the younger of the two, said:

"When Ben was so helpful and kind at the Trading Post, teaching us an honest trade like the shoe repair business that we enjoy so much, we could not help but change how we felt about families like his. Now, I like to think that Kurt and I will forever be happy...and honest...citizens of Canada."

*****

There was more hugging, and kissing, and shaking of hands with everyone in the room. The two men, with great big smiles, returned to their seats in the corner of the room.

As soon as they settled down in the old sofa, Lily stood up and smiled at me and our family. She said she had a few words of her own to share with all of us. She touched Julianna's hands for a second as she walked by. She blew a kiss to the children. Lily patted my shoulder as she stopped in front of me.

We could see the tears in her eyes.

She was barely able to speak:

*****

"I was a part of this, too. It seemed like a lot of fun...at first. I had lots of extra money...to buy pretty things."

Lily looked so sad. She was looking down at the floor.

"I had no idea of all the bad things that were happening to some of the families. I was not aware that the men on the trawler and those at the Trading Post were working together, taking advantage of the newly-arrived immigrants who could not come into the country legally.

"Many of them had a lot of money. All I did was steal a little from some of these people that stayed at my place. Johan or Heinz would bring them from Shawnee Bay all the way to Jamie's landing. Everyone was always having such a good time. I meant no harm."

I was in shock...listening to Lily's words.

She looked up at Heinz. He was standing next to Alex near the large wooden table. Johan went to his side and put his arm on his shoulder. Just by looking at him, I could tell Heinz was trying not to cry, but he could not help it; I thought he was now a changed man-- just by listening to Lily and our friends.

Lily wiped her eyes again and then looked at me.

"I have a Hungarian woman working in my diner downstairs. She can speak English, too. Julianna was talking with her shortly after they arrived two days ago. It was then that I found out what Heinz...and Johan were doing to these people. I was shocked to hear these terrible things.

"From now on...my rooms...and our meals...are free to all newly-arrived immigrants! Bless them all!"

Lily pointed at my wonderful wife.

"I have one last thing to say. From this moment on, her name will be 'JULIE'!"

*****

Alex hurried from the back of the room while we were wiping our eyes and hugging Lily. He coughed politely and looked at Julie

169

and me. Alex took a deep breath. He could not hold back the tears:

*****

"I knew the minute I met Ben and his wife that they were very special people. He added a new business to my Trading Post by teaching the art of shoe-making and repairs to Carl and Kurt. Since that time, our business has doubled. I will be forever grateful. That is the main reason I presented Ben with a new black suit. Did anyone notice? He earned it."

Alex smiled at us, sitting in the funny curved row of seats. He winked at Julie. He was a bit more composed by now.

"But that is not what I wanted to say. What I have to say is really rather simple. I only want to repay this wonderful family for all they have done for me...and the people whose lives they have touched in their new country."

Alex took a wrinkled piece of paper out of his pocket.

"I wanted to help them in any way that I could. That is why I contacted my good friend, Andrew Nagy, who works on Ellis Island. He said he had already contacted their relative who lives in New York City. He told them that Benjamin and his family could not be processed through Ellis Island. Nagy also told him that he did not know where the family was at that time.

"When I told Heinz about this sad news, he asked me to give him their Uncle Tobias' address.

"At first, I was not sure if that was what I should do, but Heinz assured me that I would be doing the right thing...so I gave him the address last week."

I looked at Julie and saw the concern on her face. I took a quick look at Heinz. I was surprised to see him smiling.

Alex waved at us and spoke in a loud clear voice:

"Now...as you will soon learn...I am sure I made the proper decision. And without further ado...I want to present to you all, my wonderful friend...and yours, also —Heinz!"

*****

Heinz walked from the back of the room very slowly. We were sitting in our curved seats again at the front of the room. Heinz stopped across from Pauley who was in the middle seat. Then he took a moment to gaze at my beautiful American family. I could see that he was holding back the tears.

For some strange reason, Heinz did not seem to be the same man that we traveled with on the trawler. He had a certain sparkle in his eyes that I had never seen before.

Heinz began to speak, very slowly…and clearly:

*****

"I never had a family of my own…or a woman I could truly love. I served in the German Navy when I was very young. That was where I earned this gold tooth of mine."

He smiled when he said those words; this was the first time I ever heard him say something humorous. Heinz does indeed look, and sound, like a different man.

"When I came to this country years ago, I was lucky to find a small job on a trawler. The owner told me he was using it to take people on sight-seeing trips around the New York harbors. I soon found out that he was taking illegal immigrants to different parts of Canada and the United States. When he took the immigrants far enough away, where they could not get back to any major ports, he left them to fend for themselves, but not before taking what little money these poor people had. This man was getting rich. He was a good teacher.

"I found out later that the man did not own the trawler; he stole it from the original owner. This man was a liar…so I 'borrowed' the trawler from him."

Everyone in the room was so quiet you would hear a pin drop. Heinz came over to me…and put a hand on my shoulder and looked at all the people in the room.

171

"I could not believe it at first. How could this one family change me and my men?

"I heard the reports about Johan—how he seemed to, ever so slowly, become a member of this family. Later, as I watched him and these people myself, I learned what it means to be part of a beautiful caring family.

"Then I realized that most people are like Ben and Julie...not trying to steal or hurt anyone—only to be helpful and kind. I found out, the hard way, how happy it has made me and my men. All the money in the world will never bring me the happiness I have felt these last few weeks. I can see that...God ...truly blesses. I had no choice anymore."

Julie whispered in my ear that she never thought we would ever see tears of joy in this man's eyes.

"From that moment on, we have been trying to help these people who cannot come into the country through Ellis Island. We are doing it with a newly discovered love for all people...and doing it without their money. My men and I want to help these people find a better way of life."

Lizzie stood up and asked Heinz if he will be her Uncle, too. We found it hard to cry and smile at the same time...but we loved every moment of it.

"I have only three more things to say. First of all, everyone here tonight is invited to a special surprise party downstairs in Lily's Restaurant. This party is a gift from Johan, myself, and all of our men. And secondly, before the night is through, we want to give back all the money we took from this family...so they can start their new life in New York City."

Paulie stood up and yelled, 'YEEE—HAAA'!

"And now we have the final surprise for this wonderful family... the biggest surprise of them all!

"Alex and his men paid for their train ride all the way from New York City, to Garland, here in Pennsylvania. Kurt and Carl brought them here from Garland. They all arrived only a few minutes ago. Tomas and I are paying their passages, along with Ben's family, back to New York City!

"You may come out now!"

Uncle Tobias and his new American bride came out of the back bedroom. We spent much of the next hour hugging our long-lost relatives. What a wonderful ending to this once-in-a-lifetime journey.

Now...we are home at last.

*****

My first American words to Julie and the children were 'I LOVE YOU'. Now, I know, we have a lifetime of wonderful memories ahead of us. This was the end to a perfect day.

The children will always be beautiful to me,
    but I can see it in Julie's face;
        she is the one who has grown
           into our 'BEAUTIFUL LADY'.

CHAPTER 58

"MY NAME IS NAGY"

ANDREW:

I am an interpreter in the largest Immigration Building on Ellis Island. Two years ago, my first job was to keep the washrooms clean and mop the floors. Today, I am proud to say that I am an American citizen.

Now I try to see that my countrymen will get through all the tests and examinations in all the different parts of the building. Most of the time, it is very comforting work to see the people come into the country...but sometimes, I am sad when some are sick and the doctors have to turn them away.

A man named Tobias was their sponsor. He was to meet the family at Ellis Island. When they did not clear customs, he knew something was wrong. My understanding was that Tobias, after waiting for most of the day, checked with the Admissions Office. According to their records, he found that the family was turned away because one of the children was ill. That is all they told him. It must have been a very sad day for this man.

*****

I can see, eventually, if and when a family is refused admission into the United States. I also try to watch for what group of 'saviors' come forward and approach these people when they leave the building.

These immigrants, who have just been denied admission into this country, are told they will be taken into the United States by another way… perhaps not legally…but it is better than being sent back on the next ship to their homeland.

I was shocked at first when I heard these terrible stories. Now, I am so pleased…as I learned lately that Heinz is a new man. God created another miracle.

I am sure stories like this happen every day in our new world. It is a wonderful feeling to have been a small part of this beautiful transformation.

*****

I took it upon myself to send their Uncle Tobias a letter, informing him about what happened to Ben and his family. I told him that problems such as these come up every week, and are usually resolved. I tried to be as cheerful as possible.

Tobias contacted me via his new telephone as soon as he got the letter. He gave me his telephone number and asked that I contact him the minute I heard any news.

A week later, I called Tobias, and told him I had sent a Telegram to Alex at the Trading Post in Canada. I alerted Alex to the fact that Heinz brought Ben and his family to Canada, with his main purpose of leaving them to fend for themselves in this vast, but beautiful, country.

As we all know, Alex played a major role in helping Ben earn some much-needed funds by him being able to work at the Trading Post. Alex also coordinated the arrival of Uncle Tobias to meet Ben and his family at Jamie's Landing. He urged Lily to keep the children and Julie at her place, too.

This family is truly blessed…with all their new friends …in this new world.

I am so happy I could help.

Thank you, God.

THIS IS ONLY THE BEGINNING:

Uncle Tobias has a job waiting for Ben at a small shoe repair shop near his home in New York City. Above the shop is a place for the family to live.

A school is only three blocks away.

And the best news yet...the school is across the street from Uncle Tobias' home.

******

My cousin has a nice upstairs flat waiting for Ben and his family on Portland Street in Delray...if they do not want to stay in New York. Detroit is just as nice as that town.

Welcome to America!

THE END

Printed in the United States
by Baker & Taylor Publisher Services